The Riddles of Mermaid House

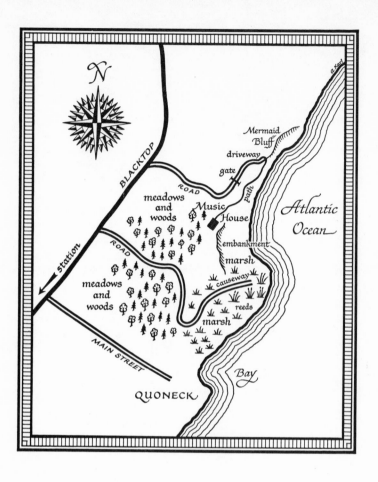

THE RIDDLES
OF MERMAID HOUSE

by Dorothy Crayder

Riddle me, riddle me,
Riddle me ree.
It's all as strange as it can be.
Who is X? And who is Z?
And what did the mermaid truly see?

BECKY'S RIDDLE

ATHENEUM NEW YORK · 1977

LIBRARY OF CONGRESS CATALOGING IN PUBLICATION DATA

Crayder, Dorothy.
  The riddles of Mermaid House.

  SUMMARY: Disheartened at being a newcomer in
New England, Becky seeks solace in studying the
marsh where she encounters a number of suspicious
people, one of who may be responsible for the town's
rash of fires.
  [1. Arson—Fiction.   2. Mystery and detective
stories]   I. Title.
PZ7.C8597Ri   [Fic]   77-2863
ISBN 0-689-30579-6

Published simultaneously in Canada by
McClelland & Stewert, Ltd.
Manufactured in the United States of America by
The Book Press, Brattleboro, Vermont
Designed by Mary M. Ahern
First Edition

The Riddles of Mermaid House

one

At best, anonymous telephone calls are not pleasant; when you're a stranger in a strange place, they're downright sinister.

Becky and her parents were having their second breakfast in their new home, and all the signs were dark. Becky's father still hadn't found his good luck Greek coin; her mother still hadn't found the lid to the tea kettle; and Becky still hadn't seen anyone to talk to except a funny looking mutt named Bobo, and gulls, lots of gulls.

The breakfast was a mess: the toast had burned; the eggs were either too hard or too soft; and the water in the tea kettle had sloshed all over the floor, making little puddles.

As far as the eye could see, there were still unpacked cartons, suitcases, shopping bags, and oddly shaped bundles of homeless objects. Ants had slowed up the packing, lots of ants in lots of places.

They were eating their breakfast without conversation, as if they all had lumps in their throats.

"But it's nice," Becky's father said, after a while.

"What is?" her mother asked.

"Quoneck."

And it was nice. It was a small village on the edge of a bay. Just beyond was the open sea. There were lovely old houses where sea captains used to live, and plain little houses where fishermen used to live—and where some still did. The house they had rented was plain and small and very like the first house Becky had drawn when she was little— square, with a pointed roof. The owners liked olive drab and varnished brown wood, and all the walls were either one or the other. Fortunately, from some of the windows there was a view of a lighthouse in the distance, and gulls, and swans, and fishing boats, which helped to wipe away the brown taste of the house.

When the phone rang, they all jumped. Becky leaped up to answer it. But where was it?

"Over there." Her mother pointed to a tower of book cartons.

Leaping over two bundles and a shopping bag, Becky found the phone. Since the first night, when friends and relatives had phoned from New York to find out if they had arrived safely and to wish them luck, the telephone had not rung once. Long distance calls were expensive, and she was going to miss the long, long talks with her friend, Priscilla.

"Hello?" Becky asked.

No one answered.

"Hello, hello . . ."

There was still no answer, but Becky could hear someone breathing. Breathing was one of the things that made anonymous calls sinister.

"Who *is* it?" her mother called out.

"Say who you are, or we'll call the cops," Becky said sternly.

There was a stealthy click.

"I don't think you ought to talk that way *here,*" her mother said. "We don't want to antagonize people. Before we've even unpacked."

"Not even muggers and thieves?"

"I don't think there are any muggers here. Are there, Charles?"

"I am inclined to doubt it."

"What about thieves?" Becky asked.

Becky had a personal interest in thieves. Only a few weeks ago, in Central Park, a boy with a switchblade had softly suggested that she hand her bike over to him. The blade had been very long and skinny and shiney. She had not argued. But when he rode off with her bike, she had hollered "Thief! Thief! Thief!" at the top of her lungs. A motorcycle cop had chased the boy, who threw the bicycle down a gully and himself disappeared.

"Oh, there may be a petty thief or two. After all, it isn't paradise."

"*Now* you tell me," her mother murmured.

When her father had lost his job as a draftsman in an architect's office because people didn't have the money to build houses, he had decided to try his luck in Quoneck. Once, when he was a boy, he had sailed into its harbor and remembered eating the best down-east clam chowder he'd ever had. He also remembered a sunrise and—well, he had always wanted to go back there. Her father was an impulsive man who counted heavily on luck.

". . . and it's bound to be cheaper living there than in New York," he had coaxed.

Her mother had given in, mostly because she tended to count on his luck. (She had been as upset as he was when he lost his good luck coin.)

So he had gone job hunting. He had found a job in a boatyard in a nearby town, and an inexpensive house to rent in Quoneck.

They had begun to pack their first cartons, and the people who had rented their apartment were measuring for curtains, when the news came that the boatyard had lost a big contract and would not be needing a draftsman.

That had left them with no apartment in New York, a house in Quoneck—and badly in need of her father's good luck.

"Who could that have been on the phone?" her mother persisted. "Charles—suppose they hate strangers here?"

"Who cares if they do?"

"I care." Becky and her mother said it together.

Her mother got up from the table abruptly and began rummaging through a hamper filled with the unwashed bed linen and towels they had used their last night in New York.

"What, may I ask, are you doing?" her father demanded. "You haven't finished your coffee."

"I'm looking for the lid."

"What makes you think you put the lid to a tea kettle in with the dirty laundry?"

"What makes you think I didn't?" Her mother's head disappeared into the hamper. When she surfaced, she was clutching a picture of her grandmother in a silver frame. "See!" she said triumphantly. "Anything can be anyplace!"

And she burst into tears and left the room.

The crunching noise, as they chewed their toast, was loud.

"Some people like to move. Some like to stay put. Your mother likes to stay put. What about you, Becky?"

"Moving's okay."

"Good girl."

"Do you think she's having a nervous breakdown?"

"I hope not."

"Me too."

"But try not to upset her, will you?"

"I'll *try*. But it's hard. She upsets easy these days. So does Nina."

Nina was Becky's seventeen-year-old sister. She

had stayed in New York with an aunt to finish the school term. As for Becky, it had been decided that she would not go to school until after the Easter holidays, a matter of a few weeks.

"What's the matter with Nina?" her father asked, as if that was the last straw.

"She knows she's going to pine away here."

Her father grabbed a piece of toast from her plate and stuffed it in his mouth.

After he swallowed it, he said: "You got any idea where that coin could be?"

"I think it fell down the elevator shaft with your keys."

"For pete's sake, Becky! You're supposed to have a cheerful nature, like me."

Becky shrugged. "You asked me a question. I gave you an answer."

"Thanks. Well—let's clear the dishes and start to help her unpack."

Her mother returned.

"*Her* doesn't want any help, thank you so much. *Her* wishes above everything else just to be left alone. Quietly *her* wishes to hunt for ants, to hunt for the lid, and just possibly to hunt for places to put EVERYTHING IN PEACE AND QUIET!"

Becky and her father studied their plates.

"In that case," her father said, "I'm going to hunt for a job. What are you going to hunt for, Becky?"

"Fleabane."

"Fleabane!" her mother moaned. "Becky, why did

you have to bring that dog into the house? Why must you always pick up waifs and strays? Why? Fleas on top of ants is just too much. TOO MUCH!'

"It isn't a bug. It's a plant."

"Then why does it have such a terrible name and where *is* it?"

"In the salt marshes."

"How did you find that out?" her father asked.

"I found a pamphlet in the attic."

"Are salt marshes safe?" her mother asked.

"Why wouldn't they be safe?" Becky asked.

"How should we know? We're not naturalists," her mother answered.

And too bad that is, Becky thought. Naturalists didn't have all this junk that had to be packed and then unpacked and washed and dusted and brushed and put away. And naturalists didn't get fired from their jobs the way her father had. A naturalist's work was wherever there was nature—which was all over (including Central Park and the backyards of brownstone houses), and was forever.

A naturalist. The thought of being one herself someday became more and more appealing. Maybe she could begin today.

She fetched a bag, and into it she stuffed the pamphlet on tidal marshes, a notebook and a pencil, her father's dictionary magnifying glass, and lunch. Lunch was two tuna sandwiches, two apples, four Fig Newtons, and a chocolate bar.

Becky threw the bag over her shoulder with the

air of someone who knew where she was going and couldn't wait to get there.

". . . and do please be CAREFUL, Becky. No INCIDENTS please. And remember we're NEW people so we've got to be extra SPECIAL CAREFUL how we act. Whatever you do, DO NOT TRESPASS."

Becky wondered when her mother would stop talking in capital letters. Perhaps when she found the lid to her tea kettle.

As she got on her bike, somewhat battered from its recent experience, Becky heard their phone ring again. She braced herself with her feet on the ground and listened.

After a while she heard her mother: now the letters were a mile high: "PLEASE STOP DOING THIS WHOEVER YOU ARE. PLEASE! Or I'll . . ."

Becky waited. Her mother dropped her voice. ". . . or I'll go crazy."

Becky began to pedal. Hard.

two

As Becky rode off, she admitted to being disturbed and anxious. Suppose the telephone caller was a mad bomber or something? In New York, where violence was in the air, an occasional anonymous caller was humdrum. But here? In the land of peace and quiet?

And on the whole, it was exceedingly quiet. Even the sounds were mostly quiet, distant and romantic. A foghorn. A bell buoy. A train rushing through the night. (The engineer of one, the 7:14 in the morning, signalled a friend, a wife, someone, with a da-da-da-da de-da-da.) And gulls. They were noisy—laughing, crying, complaining; theirs was the prevailing sound of Quoneck.

But, as for people, their only sounds had been of a door slamming, the rattle of a garbage can, a car revving up at four in the morning (no doubt a fisherman, her father had said), an occasional car on their street, the soft chugging of the fishing boats as they went off before dawn and returned at twilight.

So far, Becky had seen no one but an ancient man at the little general store, Trento's, where she had gone to buy bread and milk. He had given her a smile that was elsewhere; she had said "Thanks." She guessed for the smile. And she had dawdled in front of a glassed-in counter with a good supply of red hot balls, Mary Janes, chicken feed, licorice shoe strings, and other favorites . . . which meant that children must be somewhere around. She had bought one string of licorice. "Only *small* treats," her mother had said, "until your father goes back to work." You can't get much smaller than one string of licorice. Out of her own savings, she had bought the chocolate bar.

As she pedaled through the streets, she thought she saw a hand open a curtain just enough to peer through it. The feeling of being observed was spooky. What were they noticing? That her sneakers were brand new? That her jacket was *too* red for such quiet streets? Spooky . . . People traveling through jungles must feel spooky too.

But it was pretty. And clean. And chilly. And windy. There wasn't much to show that it was the beginning of April except some tiny buds on the trees. "Spring is late here," her father explained when there was a light fall of snow the first night.

"Well, as long as it comes by the Fourth of July," her mother had said, gloomily.

In New York, her mother had been brave and cheerful about her father losing his job. It was only when they were getting ready to move to Quoneck that she began acting as if the world were coming to an end.

"And what are you going to do about your unemployment checks?" her mother had suddenly asked her father last night.

"What do you think I'm going to do? Cash them of course."

"Here? In Quoneck?"

"Why not Quoneck?"

"Oh, because—because it's bad enough to be outsiders, but to let the whole village know our business . . ."

"Tilly, it isn't a disgrace to be unemployed. But as a matter of interest—where exactly would you like me to cash my checks?"

"In—in New York." And her mother had dabbed at her eyes, which were almost constantly moist these days.

Now, riding slowly through the street where the trees and the houses were the oldest and the largest and the most beautiful, where most had plaques saying that ship masters and maritime entrepreneurs (whatever they were) and ropemakers had built them in the 1700s, Becky felt as if she were riding back into American history, back to the first Fourth of July. Built in 1780, one house said. That was only four years after the words "life, liberty, and the pursuit of happiness" were written. She bet the people who lived in *that* house wouldn't hate people just because they were outsiders and unemployed. Would they?

A very fat, very sleek, very haughty black cat squatted directly in her path and did not intend to move. He stared at her with large, cold green eyes that said: "You do not know the answer to that question or any other questions about this village because you are an *outsider.*"

"Okay, cat, you'll be sorry. I'm a very good friend to cats. Ask any New York alley cat."

But she was the one who had to give in and ride around him.

She rode through the alien quiet. "But this village is my new home," she protested. "I am an American citizen and I have as much right to be here as—as—any first settler had. More. Because I'm not killing any Indians to make room for me."

The village kept its quiet.

When Becky came to the outskirts of the village, she stopped. In front of her, a narrow blacktop ran north and south; in either direction there ought to be a way to get to the salt marshes. Becky headed north, for no particular reason, except a vague notion that the further north one went, the closer one would get to nature.

A milk truck going south passed her. The driver waved, and she waved back. That was friendly.

A large black car traveling north much too fast for

such a narrow road passed her, much too close for comfort. That was unfriendly.

Before long, she saw a dirt road going east toward the sea and took it. Taking roads as the whim struck her was a new experience. Exciting. This was a kind of freedom she'd never known. Back in New York, in the park, there were "safe" paths and forbidden ones. Citywise kids knew which were which, but even a citywise kid like her had gotten her bike stolen.

The road to the sea hovered between landscape and seascape. Sky-high elms and maple and oak gradually were replaced by pine and scrub, and rolling pastures by moorish patches.

All at once, around a bend, there was the marsh.

Becky blinked. Her city eyes had to adjust to this dazzlement of water and sky and marsh of blues, and the new greens of rippling grasses pushing through the bleached gold of winter.

And there, beyond the marsh and across a cove, stood a house. In the bright sunlight, it was sharply outlined against the sea and sky. Hugging the land in a random way, and surrounded by the sea, it was like some lovely—and lonely—piece of driftwood. A weathervane turned in the wind. It was a strange one—certainly not the usual rooster or horse. But what was it? Someday soon, she would find the way to get close to the house.

But not today. Today she was in search of flea-bane. She got off her bike and leaned it against a rock. She hesitated: No locking up? You leave your bike just like this, without anyone minding it? Like all this new beauty, safety was also going to take getting used to.

Becky stepped forth tenderly, as a stranger should, to explore the marsh. How was she going to find fleabane, whose "beautiful pink or purple heads of flowers" wouldn't be out until August? Baby leaves all looked distressingly alike to her. How to pluck the one with "serrate margins" from the "scurfy and coarsely toothed"? Oh well, she thought philosophically, she'd live and learn.

She had not gone more than a yard or so down a narrow path when she heard a scream that made her duck her head and cover her ears. In the jungle of the West Side, she had heard screams before, nighttime screams, daytime screams, the awful unreal screams of violent crime. But she had never before been *inside* a scream, enveloped by it, almost had her head taken off by it. She slowly raised her head when the sound stopped, and there, quite finished with his screaming, a few yards away a sea gull sat complacently on a hummock gazing out to sea. Becky shook her fist at it. Then she had to laugh. Since coming to Quoneck, whenever she could, she had watched the gulls glide and wheel past the windows of their cottage and had listened to their calls. They had been alluring reminders that home was now at the edge of the sea.

But what had made this gull scream so? *What?*

Becky looked and listened. All she could hear were whispers in the grasses, a flutter, a snap, something plopping into the water. Were they innocent marsh sounds?

She studied the gull with a cool eye. Then she took out a blank notebook and wrote: "April 3rd. The beginning of a naturalist. This gull has a yellow bill I would not like to tangle with. And pink legs. A gull can scream bloody murder. Do not know why. Intend to find out. People with heart trouble should be warned. Do not have heart trouble. So far. Fingers crossed."

She put the book back in her bag and walked on. Her brand new sneakers made soft, flapping sounds. They were one full size too large, to grow into because they couldn't afford to buy new sneakers every two minutes. She had had an argument with her mother about this. "I don't want my feet to grow," she had protested. "We could save even more money if we bound them up the way the Chinese used to." Her mother had won that argument by getting teary. In a way, it had been the first sign that her mother was taking the move hard.

As Becky kept on going through the marsh, her eyes became slightly weepy too. Not from nerves, but from some nameless hunger being fed at last.

Soon, she left the main path for a narrow causeway that ran through shallow water. Here, rushes and grasses grew tall in their watery beds, tall enough to hide in, Becky thought.

A small whirlpool caught her eye. A head emerged, a bird's head suspended from a long, curved neck. Crouching low, Becky crept close to the water and then stretched out flat on her stomach to watch. She lay there quietly. The bird seemed not to know she was there. After a while, she made this entry in her book: "Still April 3. Bird diving. Up and down. Up and down. Find out for what. Goosey neck. Orange throat. Me and bird all alone. Nice. Zoom! Off it's gone. Big black wings. Guess where? To a rock. To sit straight up with its wings out. Drying off, I guess. Who is this bird? Bird watching good."

Becky left the great bird sitting on a rock and follow the causeway as it curved toward the sea, until she was stopped by a sound. It was the faintest of sounds—the pitiful kind of mewing that a lost or abandoned or orphaned kitten or puppy would make.

Instinctively, really without thinking, Becky went toward it.

This was not easy. The mewing came from a wooded slope on the land side of the marsh. Becky had first to find a way to get there without removing her sneakers and wading in icy water. She spotted a place where clumps of matted, flattened marsh grass would act as stepping stones, if she could stretch her legs and keep her balance. Teetering uncertainly, she made it to the other side, happily

18

muddying her sneakers, which were badly in need of aging.

On dry land again, Becky began to work her way up the slope, which was steeper than it had looked. With damp, slippery, dead leaves and mossy stones underfoot, and thistle that stuck to her jacket, and thorns that scratched, and brambles and branches to be shoved back or crawled under, Becky thought that only a lover of waifs and strays like her would have persisted.

Or a would-be naturalist. For behind its dark shadows, the wood seemed to be teeming with secrets and clues to beginnings and endings—a dead leaf clinging to a sprouting twig, a broken egg shell, and, off by itself, a wad of feathers and a tiny head. Becky turned away from this with a shiver. Death in the animal world horrified and frightened her.

The mewing had stopped. Been stopped by death? Becky was strongly tempted to turn back, but didn't.

High up in some tree tops birds called to each other. One call prevailed: that bird was living it up, gay and indifferent to death.

Then a new sound cut that song short. And made Becky stop as suddenly as if a hand had crashed down on her shoulder. This sound was human, familiar—and not familiar. Someone was sobbing, and the sobs had a terrifying edge to them.

Becky kept on going, creeping as stealthily as

plopping sneakers and a rough surface would allow.

The sobbing had stopped. The wood was now peculiarly quiet. All in it—insects and birds and animals, and the trees themselves seemed to be on the alert, listening only to something from the outside creeping through it. And the sobber, was the sobber listening too? Waiting?

As she crept, Becky peered anxiously through trees and shrubbery, not really knowing which way to go. Once the sobbing had stopped, Becky was no longer certain where it had come from. It was as if the wood were conspiring to keep it a secret. And Becky began to wonder if it had not been just another gull playing some gullish—or ghoulish?—trick.

Then she saw the tree.

It was like a tree out of a strange dream. Bleached, charred, with all its branches partially amputated, it stood, lonely and bereft, overlooking marsh and sea. More dead than alive, it's ancient trunk and wounded branches still sprouted new budding twigs, pathetically, like some ridiculous old woman wearing teenage clothes. It stood there telling of hurricanes and great winter storms and bolts of lightning, telling of violence it had survived.

The sobber had stopped sobbing, and up ahead the weird tree beckoned, and Becky responded.

She had gotten through the last of the brush and was almost at the edge of the clearing around the tree, when she saw the old woman squatting on the ground. Another foot or two and she would have been on top of her. She was leaning forward, toward Becky, and in her gloved hand an object glinted.

Although the old woman's eyes were hidden by old-fashioned, mauve-tinted glasses, Becky could feel them staring at her. At that moment, these eyes had a mysterious, malevolent power that kept Becky from fleeing.

three

The glinting object in the old woman's hand also kept her from fleeing. It might just possibly be a knife that would land in her back.

The old woman was whispering. It was like the whispering of some ancient instrument, long unused and belonging to a ghostlike past. But why was she whispering? Becky looked beyond her, around the small clearing. There was no one there.

"Answer me . . . please . . ." the old woman was saying.

"I'm sorry, but . . . I . . . I wasn't listening."

The mauve glasses remained fixed on her.

"No one ever does. Anymore. But at least you admit it. What I said was, *who* sent you?"

The woman had raised the hand holding the object. Becky was relieved to see it was a trowel, but she ducked all the same.

"No one sent me."

The old woman stabbed the ground with the trowel with an amazing display of strength. There was about this woman a strange combination of strength and frailness. Her small head with its close cropped thick white hair and an arrogant, aquiline nose was a feisty patrician's. She was wearing a pale grey turtleneck sweater, and a foreign-looking, green lodencloth cape fell from her shoulders and lay in a semicircle behind her.

"Now, you must listen to me," she ordered. "I don't know who you are, or where you came from, but you must listen because there is something you must know." Her papery thin body began to tremble, as if someone, or something, were shaking her. "You must not lie to me. Did you hear that?"

Becky nodded.

"That's better. You see, lying to me is getting to be more and more—well, more and more dangerous." There was an alarming crack in the whispering that was like metal grinding against metal.

Becky turned, now meaning to flee.

"No! Not yet! Am I frightening you?"

"Uh—" Becky spoke over her shoulder, one foot ready to go, "you see, we're new here, we just moved in and—you see, honestly, I'm awfully sorry if I trespassed or something—" It didn't matter what you said as long as you kept on talking without actually letting a dangerous nut know how scared you actually were. Until you could get hold of a cop. Only there were no cops here. "All I was really doing was trying to find some fleabane . . .'

"Yes, you are frightened. But then—so am I—" The woman whimpered softly, and Becky knew she was the whimpering, sobbing creature. Knowing this was no comfort. This sort of dashing old woman did not look like the whimpering, frightened kind. "You see . . ."

Becky waited for the old woman to go on. For the first time she noticed the remains of a stone foundation and a fireplace. Then, had a house once been here? This ruin, with the weird tree standing beside it, gave the little clearing an indescribable air of otherness, of a whispering past, of dark secrets.

"You see only we knew *that* way up here, and besides, it's all overgrown, isn't it?"

"I guess so."

"Then what—or who—*made* you?"

Lying was dangerous, she had said. "I . . . I heard someone crying . . ."

"Ah-h-h!" The old woman took a deep breath. "You heard a cry and you went to it—over hill and over dale through the darkness of night. Tell me, tell me do you always do that?"

The old woman was too intense, too interested in the answer.

"Why don't you answer? Is it because someone *did* send you, sent you to spy on me?"

"No, no. I told you no one sent me. I promised not to lie, didn't I? I mean you don't have to be a Girl Scout or a heroine to want to help something that's crying—specially if it's a little animal."

The woman drew herself up. "*I—I* sounded like a little animal?"

"Yes."

She passed her ungloved hand across her face, a hand Becky knew to be deceptively fragile looking.

"So it's come to that," she said, low. "Well . . . I have a favor to ask you—" she stopped abruptly.

Becky's heart sank.

"I don't ask favors easily. And this . . . this is too complicated to explain. But the favor's simple enough. Really, it's a very small one, and shouldn't put you out at all. Or certainly I wouldn't ask it. It's just that it would be kind, yes, kindhearted, if you would continue to pretend I'm a small animal, one who needs *desperately* to be left alone in peace and quiet." She looked up at the tree. "Peace and quiet here? *Here?*" She turned back to Becky. "Would you mind very much not telling anyone you saw me here? There really is no reason for anyone to know, is there?"

It was then that Becky noticed the shovel and the patches of earth, still winter hard, that had been hacked every which way. She averted her eyes hastily, but not hastily enough.

"I always was an impatient gardener." the old woman said. "Now then, are you going to be kind? Or am I asking too much of a stranger?"

Becky had a great need to see the old woman's eyes. Were they the crazy kind—or the evil kind?

"Oh, do what you want. It isn't a little favor at all. It's big, too big for a child. What I'm really asking for, I suppose, is to have one friend—*one* friend—here. Run along now. I'm tired. Asking favors is tiring. If it's fleabane you're really looking for, don't come this way again."

"I won't. I'm sorry . . ."

The old woman was no longer listening to her. She was looking at an old gold watch pinned to her sweater.

Becky began her descent, but when she was safely screened by brush she peered through it to the clearing. The old woman was creeping stealthily toward the shovel. It was almost a caricature of guilt.

After sliding, scrambling, and stumbling down the hill, Becky collapsed on the side of the bank.

Had the whole scene been imagined by her? "Becky is an imaginative child," more than one teacher had written on reports. Her friend Priscilla had also been called an imaginative child. Together they had formed an exclusive club called the I.C.C., which stood for Imaginative Children's Club. The membership was restricted to themselves and its sole purpose was to imagine. They had imagined themselves back into various centuries and into various roles, ranging from foundlings to goddesses and including spies, gangsters' molls and unwed mothers. Sometimes they had imagined themselves into a gothic tale so scary they had given themselves real nightmares.

Unhappily, in spite of appearances, this old woman was real. And what to do about it?

When in doubt, Becky ate . . . something, anything. Now, it was a Fig Newton. The Fig Newton, however, did not lead to an answer, only to another Fig Newton. It was much too early for lunch, but before she could stop herself, Becky had eaten her whole lunch, with the exception of the chocolate bar. The will power it took to save that came from not wanting to go home in need of another lunch. These days, her mother's budget would allow for only one lunch per person.

The lunch did a fair job of quieting her down, and she tried to take stock of the situation. So the old woman was a nut. What was new about that? Nothing. On the West Side, nuts were a dime a dozen: they carried crazy signs, they talked to themselves without stopping, they yelled crazy talk at you. One crazy old lady, known locally as Fanny the Phoner, used the telephone in the drug store booth once or twice a day to yell at a relative. She was crazy, but had good manners. She always asked permission to use the phone, and the druggist always gave it. Then she would march off to the booth and give this relative, someone named "Tootsie," a piece of her mind at the top of her lungs. When she was finished yelling, she looked very peaceful. She thanked the druggist; he told her she was welcome. The crazy part was that she never dialed a number; she yelled into a dead phone. But Becky thought that this craziness had some sanity to it. At least it was good and cheap.

Becky was suddenly lonely for these nuts. They weren't scary, they were just sad. And not one of them had ever asked for her friendship. Most of them lived all alone in the rooming houses that filled the side streets, where maybe their craziness was the only company they had to comfort them in their loneliness. She, for one, felt they should be allowed to enjoy it undisturbed.

But this whispering old woman was scary. What was she digging for? Or—horrid thought—what was she burying?

Try as she would, Becky could not keep her mind on nature. Granted, this was the most beautiful world she'd ever been in, and granted she didn't suppose crazy old women were lurking behind every bush, still she was filled with uneasiness and began to meander back to her bike. Meander, not run.

Gulls wheeled overhead, as if they were escorting her. Presently, there was a commotion in the sky. Rushing northward, a flock struggled to form a v. Long necks were stretched toward some destination with a kind of desperation. Geese! Becky knew them from pictures.

She pulled out her notebook: "Geese! They fly where they're going like their hearts are busting to get there. The gulls have to make way for them. Geese don't look dumb to me. I love them."

When she closed her notebook, Becky's heart stopped, and she gasped.

A man was watching her.

"You scare easy," he said.

"I—I didn't used to," Becky muttered, her voice quivering.

The man's eyes were on the notebook in her hand. Her eyes dropped to his shoes. They were black and shiny except where mud had splattered. They weren't shoes meant to walk a marsh; they were meant for city streets, fancy city streets.

"You live here?"

The man's voice was hard and shiny like his shoes. And peculiarly threatening.

"Where?"

"Here. In Quoneck."

What business was it of his? But what harm in answering?

"Yes. We're new here."

"Oh, yeah? In that case . . . you wouldn't know . . ."

He started to walk on. No thank you. No goodbye. It was as though he had been talking to an insect. Then he turned sharply.

"You all alone out here?"

Becky froze. Think fast!

"I—I'm expecting some friends—"

He eyed her suspiciously for a frighteningly long

29

moment. Then he went on his way without any comment.

Nothing had happened. But now the uneasiness she had been feeling turned into unreasonable fear.

She began to run.

When she saw the large, shiny, black car parked near her bike, somehow she wasn't surprised. It went with his shoes. So did the way he had passed her on the road.

It was the license plate that astonished her. It was from New York, and it had the letter Z on it. The plate read: 797–ZOK.

Becky knew all about Z's on New York license plates. The Z showed that it was a rented car. Movie stars and rock stars and ordinary millionaires rented these huge shiny limousines to ride around the city, and they were driven by liveried chauffeurs who hopped in and out to open and close doors for them.

Where was the chauffeur? And wasn't this a long way to come in a rented Z car for a walk in the marsh?

Becky pedaled home as fast as her legs could pump.

Who was this rich Z creep?

Whoever he was, she didn't want to meet him again when she was alone. She wanted him to drive that Z car right back to New York. And stay there.

four

Becky was not good at keeping secrets. She thought the best part of a secret was the telling. "I know something you don't know . . ." Now, all at once, everyone was asking her to keep her mouth shut about something. Of course, there was really no one here to tell a secret to except her parents, and they surely didn't need any more worries at the moment. So, much as she wanted to tell about the old woman and about the Z man, she didn't.

Particularly, since by the time she got home her mother was in a wild-eyed tizzy about noises. Didn't Becky think the furnace sounded FUNNY? As if it might EXPLODE? Oughtn't they pull the emergency switch if they KNEW where it was?

"I know where it is. It's there." Becky pointed to a red switch hiding behind a stack of cartons.

"Why didn't someone tell ME?"

"I guess you never asked."

"Oh. Well—what should we do? Listen to it. Doesn't it sound LOUD?"

Becky shrugged. "I don't know how it's supposed to sound."

"Becky, stop being so SENSIBLE and tell me what to DO."

"Call the furnace man."

Her mother glowered at her. "Don't you think I thought of that? But I don't want to start off here as a city dope."

"I'd rather be a dope than blown to bits."

"Don't SAY that. Oh, Becky, Becky, Becky, what is the matter with me?"

"You lost the lid to your kettle."

Her mother nodded as if that made good sense. Then, she asked Becky to listen to the refrigerator. Did it sound NORMAL?

Becky put her ear to the refrigerator door, tapped it, and said, "Stick out your tongue and say 'Aah!' " She shook her head. "This refrigerator is suffering from a bad case of malnutrition. I prescribe a diet of frankfurters and sauerkraut, hamburgers, peanut butter and jelly, and . . . and bagels. Lots of bagels."

Her mother closed her eyes and whispered, "Bagels. Sunday morning. Bagels. Cream cheese. Lox. New York. Oh . . ."

Becky saw her mistake and hastened to correct it.

"Daddy says we're going to dig for clams."

Her father walked in at that opportune moment.

"You bet we are," he said.

"I don't like the way you're saying that," her mother said, a note of genuine fear in her voice.

"I'm just kidding. But you didn't expect me to come back with a job the first day, did you?"

"How does it look, Charles?"

He shrugged. "Polite. That's how. I saw Adams. He owns the boatyard in the village."

"What's he like?"

"I told you—polite. What difference does it make what he's like? He had no job for me."

"But he's the first person you've really talked to since we've been here. So I'd like to know a little bit about him. I'd like to know a little bit about *anyone* here. Is that unusual? So far it's like living in shadowland with cold, gray shadows."

"I'll tell you what I know. It's not much. We didn't have much of a conversation. Adams is neither cold, nor hot. Tepid, I'd say. He's a New England gentleman—looks the part and speaks the part—who is reserved with strangers. My guess is he's warm enough with his close friends, perhaps even a jolly good fellow. I gather he's a highly respected citizen and it's considered an achievement in these parts to make the Adam's guest list. End of what I know about Adams."

"And how did you gather this much while not getting a job? Surely not from Adams?"

"Eavesdropping. The secretary was having a gossip on the telephone. And what kind of a morning did you have, Becky?"

"Interesting."

"Good girl. Find your fleabane?"

"Not yet."

"Everything takes time." His shoulders sagged, as if time was going to be too heavy for him.

Her mother kissed him on the cheek.

Waifs and strays, waifs and strays, wherever you looked.

"Hey, how would you people like to hear something good?" Becky asked.

Her parents smiled at her.

"Well—marshes are beautiful. Golly, they're beautiful, and they're right here, and it's not a big deal to get to them. You don't have to send away for tickets or passes and you don't have to pay any fare. It doesn't cost a penny."

Her parents thought that was good.

"And! I saw a house! A beautiful seafarer's house. Way off by itself. I mean really by itself. And it looked sort of silvery. And I've got to find the way to it. Somehow, I've just got to. And I will."

"A seafarer's house, eh?" Her father perked up. "And a haunting house too, it seems. Every once in a long while there is a house that grabs you, that you dream about . . . I'd like to see it myself . . ."

"Oh, maybe sometime you will." Becky said, airily. She wasn't ready to share that house with anyone yet.

AT TWO o'clock that morning a siren sounded. It tore right through a dream Becky was enjoying, one about everyone loving her at a party. In her sleep, the interruption angered her.

When she woke up, she thought the siren was the alert for a nuclear explosion, and she went flying to her parents' bedroom. They all bumped into each other in the dark hall.

"Oh, is it happening? Is it?" Becky cried.

"For pete's sake, it's only a fire." her father answered.

"ONLY a fire!" her mother exclaimed. "One match and this whole village can go up in flames. Do something, Charles!"

"If you two will shut up and let me find the chart with the fire alarm signals, we'll try to figure out where it is. Start counting the blasts."

That wasn't as easy as it sounded because of an echo. Becky thought it was blowing two long and two short, which would make it twenty-two, and her mother thought it was four.

Her father found the chart, and they settled on twenty-two, which was the town fishing dock.

The siren kept on blowing, and they could hear cars racing off.

"Volunteer firemen," her father explained, heading for the coat rack.

"Charles! You aren't planning to be some kind of hero, are you?"

"I'm planning to put a coat over my pajamas, stick

my head out the door, and see what I can see. Is that all right with you, Mathilda?" When her father was angry at her mother she was Mathilda, otherwise she was Tilly.

"Yes, Charles." Her mother was hurt.

Over and over again, the siren persisted in its call for fire fighters. Becky moved closer to her mother.

"Volunteer firemen are trained, Mathilda. They are not just guys with big hearts and little pitchers of water." Her father was slipping into his storm coat.

"I wonder if it's all right," her mother murmured.

"If what's all right?" Becky asked.

"For him to go out that way with his pajamas sticking out. I mean in this village."

Her father stamped out the door.

Becky and her mother also tried to see what they could see. They peered out various windows. They saw lights popping on in one or two houses. "Some people can sleep through anything, lucky devils," her mother said.

They saw the lighthouse beacon endlessly flashing its three reds and one white to ships that passed in the night.

They couldn't see any sign of the fire.

"I don't think the village is going up in flames tonight," Becky said. "But could we have some cocoa anyway?"

"That's a good idea," her mother said, rummaging around the kitchen counter.

"The cocoa's in the cupboard."

"I know that. I haven't lost my mind altogether. I'm looking for my marketing list."

"Now?"

"Yes, now. While I remember it. We've got to get fire extinguishers. Lots of them."

"And ropes. And ladders. And hatchets. And buckets. And . . ."

"Go on, go on, make fun of me. See if I care. I just hope for your sake that the day doesn't come when you have to admit that your mother, the nut, saved your life with her silly fire extinguishers."

"What about yours and Daddy's and maybe Nina's lives?"

"For the purpose of this discussion they don't count. Let's have our cocoa."

The cocoa was good, and Becky began to enjoy herself.

"Ma?"

"Mmn?"

"You sure make good cocoa."

Her mother regarded her over the rim of her cup.

"Thanks. Now I'll give you a compliment."

"Oh, boy."

"You have very good taste."

"Thanks."

They smiled at each other. They knew what they had wanted to say and didn't.

Becky's father came back.

"Did you see anything?" Becky asked.

"The dock's too far away. Just a faint glow in the sky."

"Is everything all right?" her mother asked.

"Mnn . . . yes."

"Okay, it isn't. What's the matter?"

"Who said anything's the matter? Any cocoa left?"

"Charles! You know how nervous it makes me to be protected from bad news. What's the matter?"

"Listen, you two, I've got to tell you something about life in a small village. Gossip isn't just a pastime, it's one of its conditions. So what you've got to do is keep your ears sharp, your mouth shut, and your mind wide open. Everything you hear isn't necessarily so. Not by a long shot."

"What did you hear, Charles, that you didn't like?"

"It seems there have been a few fires too many lately."

"Here in this village? In this firetrap? ARSON?"

"Shh! There's something else I've just learned. There's some kind of residence requirement before you're allowed to hear gossip or, of course, allowed to transmit it."

"What are you talking about?"

"They shut up when I came too close. Gossip is strictly for old inhabitants, not for newcomers."

"Oh. Burning to death is? How are we to protect ourselves if no one tells us ANYTHING? I never heard of anything so unfriendly in all my life. And they say New Yorkers are heartless. Charles, did you manage to hear whether there is a suspect?"

"That's when they really shut up. And quite right they were. You can't go around accusing people of arson. Or suspecting them of it. Publicly."

"Who are they suspecting?"

"I think some woman."

"A woman? Isn't that unusual?"

"Come to think of it, I believe it is. I'm no expert, but I don't ever remember reading about or hearing about a woman arsonist."

"Nor do I," her mother agreed.

"Becky," her father said, "your cocoa's getting cold."

"Oh? Oh, yes."

But Becky was seeing a ruin and a weird, charred tree. This would have been the moment to tell, but she didn't. "One friend," the old woman had said. "*One* friend."

five

The next day, Saturday, Becky made her first friends in Quoneck. They were a boy named Van and a girl named Clarissa, and they met at Trento's at the candy counter, over a Tootsie Roll. The three of them each wanted one, but there was only one left.

"Let her have it," Clarissa said to the old man.

"Yeah," Van grunted.

Becky found this politeness slightly chilling.

"Let's toss for it," Becky suggested.

Van and Clarissa eyed her suspiciously. That was more like it.

"Three can't toss. Only two." Van was contemptuous.

Becky blushed. "Then let's draw."

The old man let them use a straw, which they broke into three pieces of different lengths. Long was to win. Clarissa won.

"Gimme a bite," Van said.

"No way," Clarissa retorted. "You want one?" she asked Becky.

Should she? Or shouldn't she? What were the rules here?

"No thanks," Becky said.

Clarissa didn't push it.

"What you going to get instead of the Tootsie Roll?" Van asked.

"I don't know," Becky said.

"Me, I'm going to get a big Hershey."

"Big shot," Clarissa said.

They watched while Becky got two shoe strings, watched her fumble as she counted the pennies. She wondered whether their fathers were out of work too. You couldn't tell by the way people dressed; everyone dressed to look poorish, which sometimes cost a lot of money. In New York, sometimes you could tell who was rich or poor by their teeth. Braces cost a fortune. Fortunately, she didn't need any. Or by their bikes. Unless they were stolen. On the other hand, some people put every cent they had into their kids. Here she was, thinking about money again.

"I saw a funny bird yesterday . . ." she ventured, as they moved toward the door.

Clarissa and Van looked bored. Becky blushed again; that had been a dumb way to begin a conversation.

"We don't have any funny birds here, do we,

Van?" Clarissa asked.

"Yes, we do, plenty of them. And one's a firebird."

That made Clarissa laugh.

"My mother said that after last night they sure better come and get her and put her away where she can't . . ." With a glance at Becky, she stopped short.

"My parents say they never heard of a woman arsonist . . ." Becky wanted to join the conversation and also hoped to get some information.

"Oh, she's a rare bird all right." Van said.

"And experienced," Clarissa added.

"Experienced?" Van screwed up his face, puzzled.

"Dummy. You know."

"Oh. Sure. Once a firebird always a firebird."

By the way they looked at each other, and not at her, Becky knew it was hopeless to ask them to explain themselves.

"Too much talk no good," the old man said.

Van led the way to the door.

Out on the street, they headed toward their bikes. Becky wondered how Clarissa and Van were going to spend their afternoon. Whatever they were going to do, it wasn't going to include her; that was plain. Until she met them, she had intended to hunt for a way to the haunting house, a way that would avoid the ruin, and, it was to be hoped, another solitary meeting with the Z man. For the time being, the marsh was going to be out of bounds.

Now, all that mattered was to be included. What if she had told them she knew a secret they didn't know? Would that have been allowed an outsider like her?

She wheeled her bike forward. "Bye . . . ?" she called out, with what she knew sounded too much like a final plea to be included.

They didn't hear her.

Then Van looked at her bike, not at her.

"Hey!" he shouted. "Your mudguard's bent."

"I know. It happened when I was mugged."

"You were what?"

Van and Clarissa pushed their bikes toward her.

"Mugged. In Central Park."

"Wow!" They were awed.

"Are you kidding us?" Clarissa had narrowed her eyes.

"Of course not."

"Tell us about it," Van said.

"Here? On the street?"

"Sure."

Becky took a big breath. "Well, you know Central Park, don't you?"

They didn't.

"You don't know *Central Park?*"

"No. Do you know Harlan's Cove?" Clarissa was cool, very cool.

Becky bit her lip. "No."

"We've never been to New York," Van said.

"You haven't?" That was hard to believe. It

wasn't that far away.

"Millions of people haven't been to New York. They do okay." Clarissa didn't let you get away with much.

Becky took another big breath. "Well anyway— about Central Park—it can be dangerous . . ."

Becky told them about Central Park. She told them about her personal experience with a mugger. It was not the first time she had told this story so she had had a chance to polish it. The knife had become somewhat longer and sharper in the telling and this time she was careful to be extra generous with the details. "Don't forget to tell about his blood," Priscilla would remind her, and then Becky would say, "You've heard about cold-blooded murderers. Well, this mugger's blood was so cold, he looked frozen with it, more like an icicle than a boy. I thought I was about to be dead." Then she would pause and repeat: "Dead. In the afternoon. In Central Park. With people playing ball. And walking dogs. And kids. And selling pretzels." "How come you're not dead?" she had been asked once or twice. She never would answer, because as far as she was concerned it was a private matter between her and God.

When she was finished with the telling, Van was impressed. Even Clarissa was. In fact, they were the most impressed of anyone she had ever told the story to.

"I bet you're glad to be safe in Quoneck," Clarissa said.

"Safe?" Becky thought of an arsonist on the loose in a village that could go up like a match stick, but held her tongue. People get funny about their home towns. "Oh, sure."

"Mugged? Boy, oh boy, oh boy." Van's amazement was mixed with a certain amount of admiration. Then, casually: "We're on our way to the C.C. Care to come along?"

If the C.C. had been the salt mines of Siberia, Becky would have accepted the invitation. It turned out to be the Community Center, where there was an auditorium, a gym, pin ball games, ping pong tables, and candy and coke machines.

A group of boys and girls in various attitudes were having a discussion in the lobby. Some were sprawled on the floor, some leaned against a wall, one rode a bannister, one stood on her head.

"Medino's fighting mad."

"You bet he is. His net burnt up, didn't it? You know what a net costs?"

"More than Medino's got."

"No net, no fish."

"He shouldn't have called her a crazy nut, not to her face."

"What are you talking about? She went through the stop sign, didn't she? And almost hit him, didn't she? He had a right. Besides, she is a crazy nut."

"And just because a guy calls you a crazy nut, doesn't mean you got to set his boat on fire."

"Unless you're the kind of crazy nut who's crazy

about setting fires."

All eyes turned to Van, Clarissa, and Becky.

Van waved his thumb at Becky. "Her name's Becky. She was mugged."

The girl who had been standing on her head righted herself. Everyone else remained still as statues.

"Is Van telling the truth?" the girl asked.

Becky nodded.

There was a round of whistling.

"*Mugged?*"

They all crowded around Becky. They were curious, excited, some were skeptical. They were neither friendly, nor unfriendly.

"Wait till you hear about it," Clarissa said, proud to have heard it first.

Becky was not keen about retelling her story this soon. But knowing that, in a way, it was an initiation into this new group of kids, she intended to give it all she had.

"Well, there's a park called Central Park . . ." she began, this time attempting to be diplomatic.

"We know about Central Park," the girl who had stood on her head interrupted.

"*Peg*-gy, let her tell her story and stop showing off."

"She can't stop, because her head's blown up from all that standing on it," a boy explained.

"Aw, shut up," Peggy retorted.

"Yeah, shut up everyone and let her tell the

story," Van bellowed. "For those who aren't smart alecs like Peggy, Central Park happens to be a dangerous place. Okay, Becky, take it from here."

Becky had never before had to cope with an audience this distracted and skeptical. She swallowed hard and began. "So you know there is a Central Park. Well . . ."

Although this telling was not up to her usual standard, she could see that, if nothing else, they had stopped horsing around. By the time she was finished, they had gathered close to her and were listening. Then the questions began: How old was the mugger? Was he masked? Does she believe in capital punishment? Did her heart stop beating? Did she scream? Can they see the newspaper story about it? (Reluctantly, she had to explain that the papers hadn't covered this mugging because she hadn't been killed or been critically wounded.)

She was still feverishly fielding questions when someone in the huddle around her sounded an alarm with "Chickee! Psst!"

A door marked OFFICE opened, and the old woman came out.

There was some sputtering and some muffled giggles, some pinching, and some clasping of hands.

The old woman hesitated, then came toward them. She was wearing the same turtleneck and the same cape. Against her white hair and white face, the glasses were very dark. In the barren lobby, with its high, vaulted ceiling, Becky became aware of how stagy she looked. Even her walk, which was light and quick and unexpectedly youthful, seemed theatrical here.

Was she playing at some kind of make-believe?

The mauve-tinted glasses were directed at Becky, clearly only at Becky.

"Pray, do not stop your fun on my account." Her whispering voice had a remarkable ability to carry. "Oh, never mind—never mind that 'the words of a talebearer are as wounds.' "

"But . . ." Becky was so shocked and outraged that the old woman had thought she was telling about her that the protest just popped out.

The old woman shook her head and drifted on and out the lobby.

When she had gone, everyone spoke at once: "What did *that* mean?" "What was she saying?" "She's crazier than ever."

Only Peggy had something else on her mind.

"How come you know Miss Hendrix?" she asked.

The talking stopped.

With all eyes on her, Becky blushed guiltily.

"Know her? Me? How would I know her?" Strictly speaking, she didn't, did she?

Peggy persisted: "But it was you she was talking to."

"Yeah! That's right!" someone else said.

And Becky could not deny it. "But I didn't even know her name until this minute." That was the truth. "Who is Miss Hendrix?"

The reaction to this natural question was puzzling. When a jolly looking little girl started to say, "She's an—" she was poked in the ribs. "Don't gossip," she was scolded. And Becky knew it was only to an outsider that one didn't gossip. On the other hand, Peggy's suspicion that she already knew Miss Hendrix had taken hold. "You positive you don't know her?" a sharp-eyed boy asked. Becky's response was the merest shadow of a nod. No one was convinced.

As they broke up, Clarissa sidled up to Becky and said: "You better not get mixed up with old Hendrix. Not if you know what's good for you."

Coming as it did from cool Clarissa, there was no mistaking the seriousness of the warning.

six

Nina was due to arrive in Quoneck on Train Number 70, the Whaler, at 7:04 that evening. It was Becky who discovered that the Whaler "stops only on signal to receive and discharge passengers. If possible, please give notice to agent or conductor so necessary arrangements can be made."

The station was deserted. It was a tiny relic from the days when trains used to stop regularly at Quoneck, when they used to go up and down the New England coast throughout the day and much of the night. Now the station was boarded up and its paint was peeling and even its graffiti was old and faded. In the gloomy light of one lamp, it was a desolate place.

Becky's father had parked their new beat-up old Beetle, which the former owner had decorated with the flower signifying that he was antiwar. "Isn't it awfully . . . ?" Becky's mother had worried. "You know . . . conspicuous?" Becky had been shocked. "You mean we've got to be for war here?" "What we should be for here is the secret ballot, really secret." her mother had murmured. But she had been embarrassed.

Becky and her father paced up and down a cracked, cement platform peering into the murky twilight for signs of the train.

"Suppose the conductor forgets to tell the engineer or the engineer forgets to stop, then where will Nina land?"

"In the soup."

"Don't tease."

"Becky, the train's going to stop and—and everything's going to get better and what are *you* worrying about?"

"Who says I'm worrying?"

"I do."

Was this the time to tell about Miss Hendrix? Becky longed to, but somehow couldn't.

"Well, I've never been a newcomer before. There ought to be a book telling how to be one."

"Oh, you'll figure it out. Just be yourself, Becky."

"Whatever that is," Becky muttered.

"Did the kids give you a rough time today?"

"Uh . . . uh-uh. What time is it anyway?"

"The train is now one minute late."

From then on, every few minutes Becky badgered

her father for the time. "Where's the train? Maybe we missed it. Maybe our clocks are slow. Maybe . . ."

"Maybe you ought to tell me what's on your mind, Becky. You're not yourself."

"Neither are you or Mommy. We're all acting funny."

"That's true."

They walked up and down quietly, without talking. From the sea, some gulls still called, perhaps some laggard ones on their way to their roosting place.

When the train was already twenty-three minutes late, they heard the faint wail of the whistle. Soon there was a glow in the sky and then the huge eye of the locomotive's light rushed toward them.

And then, curiously, there was another light. Coming from one of the cars of the train, a flashlight searched a wood. Searching? Or signalling?

"What's that about?" Becky asked.

"You've got me," her father answered.

As the eye came closer and closer, like some earthbound meteor, Becky quivered with excitement. She had never met a train before, been this close to one.

"Is it going to stop?" she shouted nervously over the roar.

"We'll soon find out," her father shouted back.

It did begin to slow down and, as the locomotive slid past her, high up in his cabin the engineer waved to Becky. It was like having the clown at the circus give you a tiny part of the act. Wonderful. Becky waved back.

They scanned the cars, strained their eyes for a sight of Nina. Even Becky's father looked tense until they spotted her.

When they saw her, they ran toward her. Becky was, surprisingly, delighted to see her sister. She and Nina had a rough and tumble relationship.

Getting Nina off the train was a production. The roadbed was on such a slant that a parachute would have come in handy to make the leap from the train to the ground, or, at the very least, some steps. But there was no stationmaster here to provide them. Nina was wearing a backpack and her long denim skirt (one that Becky coveted). Two trainmen held out their arms to her. Nina was beautiful and was going to be an actress. She made a swan dive into their arms and gave them her flirtiest smile when they caught her. The trainmen flirted back, and Becky laughed and was proud. Not everyone had a nut like Nina for a sister.

After they kissed and hugged, Nina said, "What's going on here anyway?"

"What do you mean?" their father asked.

"Someone's been shooting at the train." Nina was practising stage voices: this one was throaty and dramatic.

"*Shooting?* From where? With what?"

"From a wood right here in Quoneck. And with a

twenty-two. The trainmen don't like it one bit."

"Neither do I," Becky said, in a small voice.

They squeezed into the car.

"So that's what the flashlight was about," their father said. "What did the men have to say about it?"

"They said they can't wait to get their hands on the punk—or punks—who did it."

"Are the police on it?"

"They seem to have their suspicions. What kind of a place is this?"

"Spooky," Becky murmured under her breath.

"A nice quiet little village by the sea," her father said, with a touch of irony. "But don't tell your mother about this. She's having a bad case of withdrawal symptoms, withdrawal from New York that is."

Becky's mother regarded Nina's safe arrival not only as a major miracle, but as a personal triumph for Nina.

"Darling, how did you get them to stop?"

"It was really quite simple," Nina said modestly. "The conductor saw that Quoneck was on the ticket and gave the engineer the message."

"I don't care what you say, it sounds chancy to me. Suppose the conductor forgot."

Their father went to find a parking place for their car. In this part of Quoneck, where the streets were narrow and the fishermen who originally settled there had had no need for barns or garages or driveways, parking space was not always easy to come by.

And Becky took Nina on a tour of the house.

"Pretty dreary, isn't it?" Nina whispered.

"Daddy says one day—if we stay here—maybe the owners will let us make it pretty," Becky replied.

"Have you got any friends yet?" Nina asked.

"Maybe. Perhaps. I don't know."

"I get it. Sorry I asked. You all look awful."

"Thanks."

Nina dropped her backpack in her room, and they went back to the kitchen.

"This kitchen's cozy," Nina said too brightly.

"We live in it," their mother said in a flat voice. "I mean huddle in it. At the Laundromat, they stopped talking when I came in."

Nina raised her eyebrows. "Mom, that's a non sequitur."

"I'm not so sure about that. When you're treated like a pariah, you huddle."

"Mom, you aren't getting just a little paranoid, are you?" Nina asked, with a slightly worried smile.

"Of course I am. Who wouldn't? What with mysterious telephone calls, arson, dangerous, crazy old women on the loose, who may be the one . . . Isn't that enough to make anyone in her right mind paranoid?"

"Crazy old women?" Becky asked.

"That's what they stopped talking about when I came in."

"What are you talking about?" Nina demanded.

Their mother gave her a highly personal account of the calls and the fire and concluded with, "Do you realize that one, ONE crazy old woman could turn this whole village into nothing but a pile of burning embers? EMBERS?"

Becky, her chin resting on her hand, had only been half listening to her mother, the other half was hearing the sound of sobs.

"New England," she began to whisper, "the home of the witch hunt?"

"Welcome home!" Nina rolled her eyes up. "And what are you muttering about, Becky?"

"I'm just wondering if maybe they're having a witch hunt and . . ."

"And what?" Nina was stern.

"And someone should stop them."

"Oh, no! This is too much!" Nina exploded. "I suppose that someone is going to be you?"

"Nina, you just gave me a good idea. Thanks."

"Becky! Becky, it was terribly noble of you and Priscilla to clean up Central Park—ugh! All that garbage—and to hand out pamphlets for every crackpot on the West Side, but remember the time you handed one out that blamed air pollution on international bankers and the Jews?"

"I suppose you never made a mistake in your life?" Becky glared at her sister.

"Well, I try to learn by mine. My advice to you is to leave the local witches to the locals."

"And let them burn her?"

"Mom! Do something with her. I don't think we ought to start out as a pack of New York busybodies."

"What are we going to be now? A bunch of hypocrites?"

"Yes," their mother answered.

"*Yes?* Rotten hypocrites? Do you really mean that?"

"Yes," their mother said, defiantly. "Until we're decently settled."

"I suppose that means until you find the lid to your tea kettle. And daddy's found a job. And Nina's got herself a new boy friend." Becky spoke bitterly.

Nina was outraged. "I don't want a new boy friend!" Her eyes filled. "Oh, God!" Her voice reached for the second balcony.

There was no balcony, but it reached their father as he came in the front door.

"What's going on here?" he demanded.

"They want me to be a hypocrite. Do you?"

Their father suddenly looked middle-aged.

"Yes. I want you all to be hypocrites. I want you all to pretend that this was the best of all possible moves in the best of all possible worlds. The damn Beetle's a lemon. The lights just went out, and I sincerely hope it's just a fuse." He shuffled out of the room, as if all his bones ached.

They caught each other's eyes and then hastily looked away.

"After you have unpacked that thing of yours, Nina," their mother said quietly, "I'd like you and Becky to peel some potatoes. Peel them thin." And she too left the room.

"I feel like the heroine of a Russian novel," Nina said, with a Russian accent. And she floated out of the kitchen.

"Farewell, Ninotchka," Becky called after her.

Becky remained in the kitchen and tried to think calmly, coolly. "Brainily, Becky, brainily," she implored herself.

Suppose, just suppose, she was being soft hearted—and soft headed—about someone who was criminally insane? Suppose Miss Hendrix was the one who had fired on the train? Old as she might be, with that cape and that walk, she had the air of someone capable of playing the role of a nutty brigand. And suppose she set the whole village on fire? Why didn't she want anyone to know she was up there at the burnt-out place? BURNT-OUT? And WHAT was she digging for? (Becky realized she was beginning to think in capital letters.) *"Please* don't tell anyone. *Please,"* Miss Hendrix had begged.

What she needed, Becky thought was a heart transplant from Attila, the Hun.

That not being available, she ate a Fig Newton. Munching on it, she remembered that Nina had said that the police were looking into the train incident, and they must also be looking into the possibility of arson, so why must a mere kid like her butt in?

She almost convinced herself that she mustn't.

That night three things happened, all of them bad: the anonymous caller phoned again; Nina's boy friend did not phone; and the wind began to blow. It blew from the northeast, and it blew hard. It blew in strange, erratic swirls, and incessantly.

An arsonist loose in a high wind?

Lights popped on and off throughout the village that night. That night, the people in Quoneck slept uneasily, some not at all.

seven

The wind blew all that night and all the next day, never stopping. It didn't wail; it made great, roaring noises, like flights of giant planes flying too low. Only a few gulls braved the wind, and they were swept across the sky at lightning speed, almost out to sea.

Every once in a while, it seemed as if the fire alarm was being sounded. With the wind there was no way of telling, that is not to their untrained ears.

And the house shook: everything in it shook—the dishes and the glasses that had been unpacked, the picture of Becky's great-grandmother (that Becky's mother had insisted on hanging up to make the place more like home), the window panes, the beams, and the floor boards. They had not known that a house could shake that much.

"Without collapsing?" Becky's mother asked.

Becky's father who was, after all, an architectural

draftsman by trade thought so.

"You only think? You're not positive?"

Becky's father groaned.

And Nina practised tragedy. She sat on the bare floor of her room and read aloud:

"For God's sake, let us sit upon the ground
And tell sad stories of the death of kings:
How some have been deposed; some slain in war;
Some poison'd by their wives; some sleeping kill'd;
All murder'd; for within the hollow crown
That rounds the mortal temples of a king
Keeps Death his court, and there the antic sits . . ."

Their mother came to listen, clutching a mop. Becky joined her with bubble gum blown into a huge pink ball. Nina looked terribly beautiful with her white face and her wet eyes.

"I think she may really have it," Becky's mother whispered when she and Becky tiptoed away.

"Have what?" Becky whispered back.

"Star quality," her mother replied.

But when Nina had spoken Richard's lines for the tenth time and was about to begin on the eleventh, her mother timidly suggested that perhaps Nina ought now to try her hand at something sunnier? Too meekly, Nina agreed.

" 'Hark! Hark! the lark at heaven's gate sings . . .' " she began, but now her tears flowed freely down her cheeks. Yes, Nina was showing signs of pining away.

At an early supper that night before Nina was to go back to New York, their mood was gloomier than ever and the conversation was boring: it was about fish. About when did a scrod become a cod? They didn't know. (They were eating cod. It had been the cheapest fish at the dockside market.) About how the selection was poor in Quoneck compared to New York. But fresher, their father said, much fresher.

"Joe Ferrara never gave me a piece of stale fish in his life," their mother protested. "I loved Joe."

"And he loved you too," their father said, reaching over and patting their mother.

"Yes, yes he did. He loved me. Joe Ferrara loved me." Their mother sighed. "Nina, stop in and tell Joe Ferrara that I miss him very much, will you?"

"Yes, Ma."

They picked at the cod. Their mother hadn't learned how to use the electric oven, and the cod tasted like a blotter, but they continued to pick at it.

"And tell Fanny the Phoner, that I miss her, will you, Nina?" Becky said, after a while.

"Yes, dear," Nina said. "That will give me great pleasure. And whom do you miss, Pa? That I can give the message to? Ben, the bookie? Jake, the junky?"

"That reminds me," their mother said. "Nina, please add Uncle Will to your list of people who should be told that we're alive and happy, *unbelievably* happy in Quoneck."

"You gave me Uncle Will, twice before, Ma."

"I apologize for losing my mind." Their mother pushed her plate away. "And for this—this fresh, *fresh* piece of flannel! Joe Ferrara never sold me flannel for fish in his life. *Never!*"

The others pushed their plates away and ate lots of bread.

They all went to the station to see Nina off. The train she was to take was one of the few that did make a scheduled stop at Quoneck, so there was to be no wigwagging to the engineer—a disappointment to Becky.

As it happened, it was only by fate's playing one of those split-second games, that they ever got to the station at all.

With the green light in its favor, the Beetle was turning south on to the black top, when a car traveling at about ninety miles an hour with no intention of stopping for a red light headed toward them.

Their mother did not scream. No one did. Possibly it was their fear that left them mute. And it was this muteness that may have saved their lives, made it possible for their father to keep his head, and keep the Beetle from turning over as he swung into the wrong lane.

But before the car disappeared into the night, Becky saw the Beetle's headlights pick up its license plate.

She was the first to utter a sound. It was a fusillade of Z's: "Z ... Z ... Z ..."

After her father had used some very rough language about drunken murderers on the highways, he asked Becky to tell them what that idiotic Z-ing was all about.

"It's the license plate! A New York Z license. I saw it before. Out on the marsh."

"On the marsh? A New York rented limousine? That's unusual. Did you see the driver?"

"Yes."

"What'd he look like?"

"Scary," Becky said, in a small voice.

"See!" her mother said. "I told you that maybe the marsh was dangerous. Didn't I? Maybe that's why he just tried to kill us, because Becky saw him there."

"Mathilda! For heaven's sake! How could he possibly know that Becky was in this car?"

"I don't know and neither do you. That's the whole trouble here. We don't know anything about anything."

"But, Daddy, what do you think he was doing out there? All dressed up in city clothes?"

"I don't know, Becky," he said, with an edge to his voice.

And that was the most frightening answer he could have given her.

"And whoever he is," he added, "he seems to be on his way home, so let's drop it."

This, they were all willing to do.

They pulled into the ghostlike station and waited

in the car. Although the wind was not as strong there as it had been closer to the water, the Beetle trembled.

"I wish I was going back with Nina," Becky blurted out.

"Who doesn't?" her mother responded.

"What I appreciate is a family that's with you right down the line," her father said, bitterly. "Courageous, optimistic—and patient. Did any of you ever hear of patience as a virtue?"

And he got out of the car, slamming the door violently.

"I'm sorry," Becky said. "It just jumped out."

"Poor Pa," Nina said.

"You don't have to rub it in," Becky snapped.

"Stop fighting," their mother ordered. "He's right. We're acting awful. We ought to be ashamed of ourselves. This isn't Siberia. Not really. It only seems like it. I think we should all try to act as if coming to this Godforsaken place is a thrilling adventure." She paused. "Becky, you're imaginative. Imagine us up a good adventure."

"I'll work on it," Becky said.

"In the meantime, Becky, go tell your father to come back out of the wind. Tell him we're going to be brave. And maybe even noble. But don't promise patience."

The wind itself sent their father back to the car, and they waited for the train silently, isolated in their loneliness.

When the train came and Becky saw the lighted cars filled with people, most of them young and most of them presumably going to New York, her eyes stung with tears.

Smiling and joking, two trainmen hoisted Nina up, and the three left behind stood close to each other in the blackness of the platform and waved her off. She waved back, but, in the next minute, Becky saw her smiling and talking to a young guy who was helping her with her backpack. Deserter, she thought; unfairly, she knew.

They drove home without talking. For being minus only one person, the house seemed singularly empty, and they were still silent when they drank cocoa before going to bed.

As Becky lay in bed, listening to the wind, she remembered hearing grown-ups say, "This too will pass." How did they know? And when would it pass? And would the wind ever stop blowing? And would they ever be at home here?

eight

In the days that followed, Becky remained an outsider and, in her loneliness, she tried to distract herself with nature, all of it: the land, the sea, and the sky. Excluding the marsh. Unhappily, the Z man had cast his sinister shadow over its dazzling beauty. What if he did return and found her there alone again?

"Star gazing is amazing," Becky wrote in her diary. "And uplifting (joke). But Siriusly (another joke), it is hard to believe what's been going on in the night sky without my even knowing it. A-mazing! And now right from my very own bed, with my very own supply of potato chips, which I don't have to share with greedy Priscilla, I have a view of the whole thing for *free* and *live*. No admission charge, no standing on line to get into the Planetarium at the museum. Right now, I'm guessing that that bright star is Sirius. Hello Sirius. There's one thing about this watching the night sky that's scary, really scary, and that's infinity. Anytime anyone poo-poohs infinity tell them to watch the night sky. Infinity, when you see it live, going on and on and on and never stopping is scary, I don't care what anyone says. At least for a beginner like me. The day I'm not scared of infinity is I hope when I'm about to die. I seem to be getting morbid so I better stop."

IT WAS on April 10th, that Becky met Winky. And Mr. Mills. And saw Alfie Stone for the first time.

She would never forget that date, not only because of what happened later, but because this is what she wrote in her diary: "This is about a dog because naturalists are also interested in animals. Aren't they? I fell in love with a dog. I mean I really and truly *love* this dog. Believe it or not, her real name is Champion Windermere's Duchess of York, but thank goodness her nickname is Winky. She's a Norwich terrier, which I never heard of before probably because it is such a high class type dog. She's little enough to cuddle in your arms but she's not a lap dog. She has brown rough fur and the brightest black eyes I've ever seen, and she is very gay and brave. And she loves me too. And Big News and fingers crossed, I may get to dog-sit for her for MONEY. I hope Bobo's feelings are not hurt. He brought me and Winky together. Winky belongs to Mr. Mills who is a nice man and FRIENDLY."

This meeting, which was to prove so important,

came about because Becky wanted to explore the town fishing dock and the boatyard, neither one of which she had yet seen. And Bobo felt like coming along.

On the way, she saw Alfie Stone.

That happened when she and Bobo were in front of The Gull. The Gull was a trim, red house with white shutters and a white picket fence. A sign shaped like a gull said: "The Gull" and "Guests".

A boy, about sixteen, was sauntering toward Becky and Bobo. He was looking at the ground as he walked, his shoulders hunched, his hands in the pockets of a down jacket. When he came closer, Becky saw that his face was pasty and pimpled— and sullen.

Bobo did not like him. At the sight of him, his tail went down, and he began to make low snarling noises.

Becky scolded: "Bobo! Stop that!" and grabbed his collar.

The boy barely looked at her or Bobo and said nothing, just kept on walking.

"Alfie . . ." a woman's voice called from a window in the Gull. "Alfie Stone!"

The boy turned his head sideways and kept on going.

"Whaddye want?" He too snarled.

"I want you to tell yourself and your mob that if I find another beer bottle in my yard . . ."

He grinned insolently and sauntered on. He had

not stopped for a second, and he had not taken his hands out of his pockets.

The woman shut the window. When Becky thought Alfie Stone was safe from Bobo—or, more likely, Bobo was safe from him—she released him, took a big breath, and went on.

"Wouldn't want to meet him in a dark alley," she thought.

And in a few minutes she forgot about Alfie Stone.

The town fishing dock was quiet at this hour of the morning. The catch, good or bad, had gone to market, and the fishermen to their coffee and fish talk. Some small lobster boats and some chunky draggers were moored to the piers. Empty lobster pots were piled up on the wharf next to the lobster boats, and nets from the draggers were spread out next to them. One dragger was named *Three Brothers* and one was called *QE III.* The dock was obviously cat country. Becky counted six who were either still eating fish or were sunning themselves on full stomachs. They paid no attention to Bobo, and he pretended to ignore them.

Then all at once, Bobo stood still and his tail went straight up. He made a wild charge toward a man walking a little brown dog on a lead.

Becky, thinking that Bobo, who was a big dog, would hurt the little one, ran after him, and met Winky. And Mr. Mills.

"Don't worry," the man called out. "Winky won't

hurt him." And he released his dog.

Becky saw that the man was joking, but she also saw that Winky wasn't the least bit intimidated by the large dog. If anything, it was Bobo who was.

She and the man watched as the two dogs sniffed and pawed and chased each other around.

"Are you contagious?" the man asked, conversationally. He had a pleasant, musical voice.

He was a short, trim man, perhaps forty, wearing a shabby tweed jacket and an air of benevolent assurance. He did not look like a nut. (In New York, there were a couple of nuts who were so phobic about germs and pollution that they wore surgical masks all the time, as they walked the streets.)

"I don't think so," Becky answered, warily.

"Then you are playing hooky?"

Becky smiled. "Oh, because I'm not in school you thought I'm getting over the measles or something."

She explained about their having just moved to Quoneck, and that she would only begin school after the Easter holidays. It was nice to have someone to talk to.

"Ah, so we're both outsiders," he said.

Studying him out of the corner of her eye, Becky thought that somehow he didn't seem to be as much of an outsider as they were.

Becky called Winky to her, and they became instant friends. As she cuddled the warm little dog with the rough fur, and was kissed by her, she knew she was lonelier than she had admitted.

The man began to walk toward the Adams Boat Yard.

"Have you seen the yard?" he asked.

"No, but my father did. He tried to get a job there."

"No luck?"

"No. No luck anyplace so far." She felt free to talk this way to another outsider.

The man nodded sympathetically and handed her Winky's lead. Becky took this as an invitation to walk along with him, and accepted.

The boat yard was a sprawling collection of buildings. There were a couple of hangars, where Becky could see men, mostly young and long haired, scraping and painting sailboats, and a workshop, and a watchman's hut, and a small building that said OFFICE. Beyond, in the open, sailboats and motor boats were up on wooden stocks and were still covered with tarpaulins. On the edge of the water, she saw a large, crane-like object on wheels, that was attached to a tractor.

"That's called a lift," the man explained. "It's used to get the boats into the water."

"I guess you work here."

"No, I don't." He was amused. "I'm here to try to pick up an attractive charter."

"What kind of a boat is a charter?" Becky asked.

"It's not a kind, it's what you do when you want to rent a boat. So far, Adams hasn't come up with just the right one for me—speaking of whom . . ."

A station wagon came toward them and stopped. Her father had given a good description of Mr. Adams. Becky stood to one side as the men chatted, but she could hear snatches of Mr. Adams' conversation.

". . . have an errand . . . nice sixty foot yawl . . . pictures in the office . . . drink at the house this afternoon?"

She couldn't tell whether the man accepted that invitation, but she knew she had been right: he wasn't anything like the outsiders they were. And yet, the smile he wore as he came from the exchange with Mr. Adams was just a shade too victorious for someone used to being accepted. Was he lonely too? Or, on second thought, was the smile for the nice yawl he might get?

Becky's meeting with the man ended on a surprising, and exciting, note. Would she, he wondered, care to dog-sit with Winky some time? For pay, of course? Would she ever! It was then that they exchanged introductions. Becky gave him her name and telephone number. And he was a Mr. Leonard Mills and was staying at The Gull.

Taking Winky with him, Mr. Mills went on his way to the office, and Becky floated home.

BECKY WAS so eager for her dog-sitting job, that for two days she hung around the house waiting for Mr. Mills to call. On the third day, an overwhelming yearning to find the house that continued to haunt her (and a growing conviction that Mr. Mills would never call) made her leave.

That day, she did find the way to the house. And she also found the dead birds.

Still remembering to keep an eye out for the Z man, Becky went farther north on the blacktop than she had ever gone before. It was a narrow dirt road, little more than a wagon path, and one that could easily have been missed, that led to the house. It wound in and out of pine woods, so that now she saw the house and now she didn't. It wasn't until she was nearly on top of it that she knew she was on the right road.

Close up, the house was even more beautiful than she had imagined. It did stand absolutely alone, and was so much surrounded by the sea that its weathered shingles and the sea seemed to have made a secret truce with each other, had become wary friends.

The weathervane made her heart turn over. It and the house belonged to each other. It too was beautiful, and romantic, and bound to the sea. It was a mermaid. A breeze off the sea had turned it toward her, and to Becky, the smile it wore was strangely secretive.

She biked down the road to get still closer to the house. Just before the road ended at a bluff overlooking a rocky shoreline, a long, winding driveway led to the house. It was bordered with windswept trees and fields of wheat-colored grass. Across its entrance, a closed gate bore a sign that said: PRIVATE: ABSOLUTELY NO TRESPASSING: THE MERMAID.

But there was no law that said she couldn't stop, look, and wonder. She was wondering what it would be like to live in such a house, imagining herself as the heroine of a gloriously romantic life, when she saw the birds. They were very small and were huddled together. One tiny head with its white, masklike face rested on the brown, feathered back of the other, as if they had died comforting each other. At first, it was as if a knife had slashed through a beautiful picture, insanely, wantonly. And she felt only shock. It was quickly followed by her usual terror of dead creatures.

Before she could flee, she heard the voice, not whispering now, but harsh and froggy:

"Oh, my God, what have you done?"

Becky swung around. Miss Hendrix was coming from the bluff, and was holding a rag in her hand. Becky's answer was to shut her eyes tight and burst into violent tears.

Deafened by her own crying, she only barely heard Miss Hendrix repeating, over and over again: "What? What? What?"

When Becky was able to control herself and opened her eyes, she saw that Miss Hendrix was bending low over the birds.

She was crooning to them; then she picked one up and cradled it in one hand. The other hand still held the rag. Becky shuddered and covered her eyes.

"Pick the other one up."

"Oh, no—no, I can't. I won't."

"And why not? Is it your guilt?"

"No! Not guilt! Not! Not! I didn't do it. I couldn't do it—couldn't—*couldn't!* Don't you see I can't even look at them?"

Miss Hendrix didn't answer. Becky waited, holding her breath. Presently, a cold, dry hand clasped hers. "Come, I shall lead you through the gate."

Becky heard a bolt being opened and closed. Whether it was the gentleness in Miss Hendrix's voice or the physical weakness in herself, Becky quite meekly allowed herself to be led.

"You may open your eyes now."

Miss Hendrix no longer held either the bird or the rag.

"But my bike—"

"I'll put it inside the gate. Go up to the house and wait for me on the terrace. I see we must talk. I will be up shortly."

Becky walked between the windswept trees; she walked in a trance.

Then this house belonged to her? to Miss Hendrix?

The terrace was like a stage jutting out to sea. It was a place for dancing, for making great flying leaps. Only not too near the edge. Looking down, Becky saw the sea crashing against rocks with wicked intention. But around the terrace, clumps of daffodils and purple crocuses defied wind and sea.

And looking off to one side, past some more meadows and woods, she saw what was unmistakably the amputated top of the tree.

Miss Hendrix came up. The rag was dangling in her hand again, pinched between two fingers. Becky got a whiff of gasoline. With that curiously young, swaying walk of hers, Miss Hendrix went back and forth, indecisively, apparently not knowing where to drop the rag.

"The garbage can? No, that won't do. That would really finish it for me. Oh, what shall I do with this wretched, stupid—" She swung toward Becky. "What is your name?"

"B-Becky," Becky stammered.

"Becky? Becky, I'm Euphemia Hendrix and I want to know exactly what you were doing at my gate. Don't look so frightened. Really, I'm not as crazy as they would like me to be. Not yet, that is. But if they keep it up, if *she* keeps it up—" She shook her head.

"I—I was just looking."

"For what?"

"For . . . nothing. I just wanted to look at the house. You see, I've been trying to find it."

"*Find* it? Why? For what reason?"

"Just—just because I love it. That's why."

Miss Hendrix stepped closer to Becky and fixed the mauve glasses on her face.

"Because you love the Mermaid? Oh, my dear.

How beautifully simple. I think I believe you." The whispering voice was choked with emotion. "Yes, I believe you. Would you stay and have a cup of tea with me? It's so long since anyone has . . . Would you?"

She could have gotten out of it, right then and there. All she had to do was say her mother was waiting for her to peel some potatoes. (Always be specific.) But she didn't want to get out of it. She wanted to know what was going on; who was doing what to whom? Besides, it wasn't as if she couldn't run faster than this old woman, even with that young walk of hers.

They entered the house through long French doors. The inside of the house was beautiful too. Airy. And uncluttered, almost empty. A grand piano, open and with music on the stand. A chaise, facing out to sea. Some blossoms in a vase. Not a room to be murdered in, so she needn't worry about *that.*

"How do you take your tea?"

"With everything please. Milk and sugar. If you have them."

"I have them." She began walking toward the far end of the long room. "I do keep up certain standards." She said this in a mocking way. "Which is exactly what *she* doesn't want me to do," she added, no longer mocking.

Who was *she?* Becky wondered, as she watched her go out the room.

A large brass telescope stood on a tripod next to the window. She didn't think Miss Hendrix would mind if she looked through it. When she put her eye to the lens, she was unnerved to find that instead of being pointed out to sea, it was pointed toward the village. The thought of Miss Hendrix spying on the village was not pleasant.

"Yes, the village. With good reason."

Becky jumped.

Miss Hendrix was carrying the tea tray. She set it down on a low table near the telescope. Becky sat down opposite her, primly, her back straight and stiff. The tea tray seemed very fancy to her with its lacy cloth, thin flowery cups, and silver tea service. At home, a cup of tea was a cup of tea, usually had in the kitchen. This tray demanded tea manners and tea conversation, the kind she and Priscilla used to make up when they went to tea at Buckingham Palace: "Your majesty, and how do you find the state of the Empire?" one of them would begin. "You look at a map." Hilarious giggles.

"I see the silver is in need of polishing," Miss Hendrix fretted.

Becky saw that Miss Hendrix was right. She also saw that Miss Hendrix's hand trembled alarmingly, and that some tea spilled onto the cloth, making an ugly stain.

Miss Hendrix set the teapot down. "But is that enough to declare me incompetent? Incapable? Dangerously insane?"

Becky held her breath.

"Is that a reason for her doing what she wants to do to me? Is it?"

"I—don't know.

Miss Hendrix leaned back, rested her head against the chair. She was wearing the same turtleneck. It was like a uniform, or costume. Becky thought she must have once been beautiful.

"My poor child, of course you don't know. How could you? Who would tell you? Certainly no one in this village. I seem now to have a terrible need to talk, and I don't want to start talking to myself. Do you mind if it's you? You do have a listening face."

Becky swallowed some tea with difficulty.

"I may repeat myself. I may weave back and forth like a distraught spider. But then I am distraught. Those birds. The rag. I put it in an empty tin in the kitchen. Someone's trying to drive me crazy. It is possible to do that you know, actually drive someone crazy. And she is behind it. She would be the one who knows how much I love the plovers. What she doesn't know is that I'm still able to walk the bluff where I found the rag . . ."

"Who is she?"

"She is my sister Hope. She was named Hope. They gave me Euphemia. Such a heavy name for a child. I always wondered what I was a euphemism for. Luke . . . Luke called me Fifi. He would. My darling Luke . . ."

"I don't know who Luke is."

Miss Hendrix was startled, as if she had forgotten Becky was there.

"Oh! How strange. I never talk about Luke. Never. But about Hope? Yes, I want to talk about her. She hates me and I hate her. We talk through her lawyer, a dreadful man. The Mermaid was my mother's house. She died shortly after Hope was born and the house was left to the two of us. If one of us was not to marry, it was to be that one's home for the rest of her life. I am the one who is not married. Hope is, and she lives in California. She never wanted me to have this house, but there wasn't anything she could do about it. She never wanted me to have anything. Our father lived here until his death. I traveled much of the time when he lived here. You see, Hope was his pet, his dearest pet. I—I—well, he always thought I was guilty, that I was the one who had done it, so it's not surprising that he didn't love me, is it?"

Guilty of *what?* Becky longed to ask, but didn't dare.

They drank their tea. Becky was impatient for Miss Hendrix to go on, get to the point of all this.

Miss Hendrix must have seen her fidget or read her mind.

"What's happening now is that she's trying to get me out of this house and into a nursing home, I suppose. She says she has a buyer for it, someone who's willing to pay an enormous price for the Mermaid. A mysterious someone whom they call X, as if it matters to me who it is. What does matter to me is that they're trying to drive me crazy, make me incompetent. And I've got to stop it! Before they succeed." She fiddled with the tea tray. "And I think I know how—if only—You didn't tell the children about finding me at the music house?"

"The music house?"

"The remains of it, the ruin, where you saw me digging."

"No, I didn't tell."

"You didn't?" She paused. "I apologize for not trusting you. You see, I'm digging for the truth. All my life I have been living with her dreadful lie about me. I was helpless—too young, too lost I guess, to fight it when I should have. Living with such a lie, the way I have, has been like living much of the time in prison . . . But now, I *must* find it!"

"Find what?" Becky asked, very low.

"The bracelet."

"Bracelet?"

"The bracelet. I see—I see that now I have to talk about Luke. Luke . . . and what happened . . ."

The story Miss Hendrix told came out like an old patchwork quilt: first one scrap, then another, plucked haphazardly from the past.

It was left to Becky to put the pieces together, pieces of a story she wanted desperately to believe.

It began with the date, as much as the place. The date was July 3rd, about sixty-five years ago, and the place was the music house. The music house had belonged to Euphemia's mother. Her mother had been a pianist, and Euphemia had hoped to be one too. (Of course, she never became one, not after what happened.) The music house had gotten to be Euphemia and Luke's house, their private place. They were both twelve at the time, and they were each other's very best friend. Luke always spent summers and holidays in the village. They both loved music and they used to play duets by the hour. Or read or play games. True, they often would lock Hope out, because she pestered them, and Hope would go screaming bloody murder to their father. And Euphemia would be punished because "Hope was only ten and she was the older one and should know better," their father would always say. Oh, the punishment was deserved of course, but Euphemia knew her father loved Hope more than he loved her, which was punishment enough.

Of course, Hope was very jealous of her having Luke as a friend. But Hope was just naturally jealous of Euphemia, which always puzzled her. After all, wasn't it enough for Hope to be their father's pet? Or was she so jealous because such a pet is supposed to have *everything?*

Euphemia thought it may have been Hope's jealousy that drove her to do what she did. Not that she meant to burn to death—that bad she wasn't.

That summery day, that July 3rd, the day before they were going to have fireworks on the beach, Euphemia and Luke had been in the music house.

They had been playing a Schubert duet, but then Luke wanted to finish the hull of a model sloop he was making. Euphemia wanted him to hunt for starfish with her. He wouldn't do it. No, he wanted to work on the sloop.

So she left him there in the music house. She had been cross with him, but he had looked up and smiled at her. No one ever smiled the way Luke did. And he had said, "Tomorrow, Fifi . . . I promise."

Those were the last words Luke ever said to her. There wasn't any tomorrow for Luke. He was burned to death in the music house.

As she had been telling the story, Miss Hendrix had prowled the room; then she stopped at the window and looked out to sea.

"Luke?" She called his name as if he were still alive.

Becky didn't know whether Miss Hendrix was finished with her telling or not. And she didn't know what to do. What to say. You didn't just say you were sorry after hearing a story like that.

Miss Hendrix spoke again:

"It goes without saying that everyone was sure I had done it. With a sparkler that had ignited the glue Luke was using. Hope, the expert liar, with such evil innocence, said she had seen me at the package of fireworks. I denied it. I had no proof though. There were no starfish that day. I had no starfish to show where I'd been. But even in my horror, as I denied what she said, I saw her empty arm, saw that the bracelet that was always on that arm was gone. It didn't really mean anything to me then. All that mattered to me was that my darling Luke was dead. I think it was a week later that our father said to her, "Love, where is your little gold bracelet?" And then she told the big lie. Sometimes, I think she lies so much she doesn't know what's true and what isn't anymore. There was no one to teach her not to lie. 'Oh,' said she, 'I was afraid to tell you, Daddy. I lost it *yesterday,* when I was swimming out where it's deep. It fell down to the bottom of the sea. Are you going to spank me?'

"But I knew she hadn't been swimming. All at once, I remembered her bare arm that other day, and I knew she was the one who had set the fire that . . . that killed Luke. I screamed out that she was a liar. Oh, how I screamed! She burst into tears, and I was sent to my room in disgrace. From that day on, our father lost what little love he ever had for me. But I think deep in his heart he suspected his pet.

"And I imprisoned myself. I built a shell around that lie . . . and lived with it, became the recluse I am today.

"Now I can no longer live with it. Now I must prove that she lied. It's like—like psychological warfare. The whole village has always believed her big lie about me, so it's easy for them to believe that I'm a deranged old woman now. And, oh yes, I myself have helped. Yes, I have been reclusive, eccentric. Yes, I did go through that stop sign. Yes, I was furious when Medino called me a crazy old woman. Yes, yes, yes to all that but, no—no to having killed Luke. You do understand why I must find the bracelet, don't you?"

"I—I think so."

"I need to be freed from that lie to fight back. Living with it *has* made me—strange. If I am suspected of arson again, I repeat—*again*—then it's smooth sailing for her. Legally, she can become the conservator of this house . . . I can be put . . . and away this mysterious X gets my lovely Mermaid."

"Oh, no!" Becky protested, as if that was the worst of the whole story.

"Oh yes, that is what would happen. I am trying to stop it, but I'm totally alone. Even the gardener has left. Didn't want to get mixed up, I suppose." She pointed to the telescope. "Yes, I've turned into a spy. I'm searching for evidence. There *is* an arsonist loose. And now the birds . . ."

Becky didn't stop to think: "Can I help?" she asked.

Miss Hendrix pressed a rib, as if she'd gotten a sudden pain.

"Help me?"

She stood still, struggling for composure.

"Oh, my dear." Her voice was choked. "You are a nice child. I can't remember when anyone last said that to me. But I can't let you. They'll think you're queer too if you befriend me. You had better not.

You're too new here for that. Only . . . if by chance you do see or hear something that would be useful, I would be grateful, of course."

Becky was too choked up herself to say more than "I will," to this proud old eagle of a woman.

As she was leaving, Miss Hendrix very quietly asked: "Tell me, Becky, do you believe the story I just told you?"

Becky felt her stomach heave.

"I—I think so," she said.

She had no way of telling whether this answer satisfied Miss Hendrix.

Late afternoon shadows fell across the driveway as Becky walked slowly down it. The boom of the sea drowned all other sounds. The wind had shifted and now the mermaid watched her as she went. She had the creepy thought that Miss Hendrix was watching too—through the telescope.

nine

Becky rode back to the village in a daze.

When she got to Trento's, she remembered that her mother wanted her to pick up a loaf of bread. Some bikes parked in front of the store made her hesitate: did they really have to have bread? She supposed they did and went in.

Clarissa, Van, Peggy, and some of the others were there, talking. They stopped when they saw her.

"Hi," Becky called, and wished she hadn't.

No one responded. They stared with eyes that were like cold stones.

"Is this a gang war or an initiation—or something?" Becky had wanted her voice to be light and cool, as if she were in on the joke, instead it squeaked.

They kept on staring at her and Peggy was the one who spoke. "You're the one who knows all about gang wars—and muggings—and crime. You tell us."

"I don't know what you're talking about."

"Sure you do. Don't play dumb."

Becky had the nightmarish idea that they thought she was the arsonist.

She backed away: "I don't know the rules of this game—"

"Okay, I'll tell you. Rule number one is don't lie to us."

This village was sure hung up on liars.

"What did I lie about?"

"Hendrix," Van said. "You told us you didn't know her."

"I didn't know her. I didn't even know her name. You're the ones who told me . . ."

"Did so know her."

"Did not."

"Liar."

"I am *not* a liar," Becky shouted, "you witch hunters you!"

Old Mr. Trento, who had been reading his newspaper in a corner behind the counter, looked up and hushed them and went back to his paper.

Van signalled them to keep quiet, and he stepped forward: "Then what were you doing at her house?"

There are no secrets in Quoneck.

"Don't bother to lie about that because the fire warden saw you through his glasses."

"Creeps! You're a bunch of spying creeps here,

sneaky, creepy creeps. I'd rather have muggers any day."

"It's his job, stupid."

"Spying on a poor innocent old woman?"

"Innocent? So you *are* her friend."

"Yes. I am. I am Euphremia Hendrix's friend. As of this minute."

Pop! Like that! No thinking! No nothing!

There was much shifting of feet. Someone snapped gum. Someone whistled softly.

"Well, well, well," Peggy said. "What was that about, 'as of this minute' stuff?"

"Just what I said. I just this minute decided to be her friend."

"Impulsive, aren't you?"

"Yeah, very. It runs in my family."

"Do you happen to know that there's an arsonist loose in *our* village?" The emphasis on "our" was cold and clear.

"I know."

"And that people might think that birds of a feather flock together?"

Becky had not thought of that. The candy counter began to spin: licorice strings and Mary Janes and hard balls all spinning wildly. Her sneakers felt hot and sweaty and miles too big.

"She is *not* an arsonist."

"Is that so? You an expert?"

"Yes."

This created a bit of a stir.

"I know more about nuts than all of you put together. I know good ones from bad ones. She is not a bad nut."

"How can you tell?" Peggy's curiosity was aroused.

"Experience," Becky bragged. "And here—" She pointed to her stomach.

If she hadn't exactly won them over, neither did they ridicule her. After all, New York was a city of nuts. And then, slightly heartened by this, Becky amplified:

"And I know she's not the one who set the music house on fire."

That was a big mistake. They became angry. Who was she to contradict a whole village of native born people who have known better all their lives? Peggy said: "Can you prove it?"

Becky was taken aback. "No! But I'm sure going to try!"

"How?"

"You'll see."

No one spoke. But as she stumbled out, she could hear the babble begin.

Riding home, her throat ached as she held back her tears. She had no intention of blubbering all over the village. She had had no intention of blubbering to her parents either, but her mother took one look at her face and shrieked: "What *happened?*"

Becky shrieked back: "I want to go home."

Quietly, firmly, her father said, "Becky, you are

home." And with that piece of bad news, Becky let go and sobbed.

Her father brought out his bottle of brandy. It was a bottle he kept for such emergencies as being fired from a job. He had had it for some years, and fortunately it was still three quarters full. He poured out a thimbleful and handed it to Becky's mother. He did not take any for himself.

Little by little, zizagging back and forth, Becky told about Miss Hendrix, about their first meeting, about going to her house, about the story she told, and about how she was now totally ostracized. Totally!

When she was all finished, her mother asked for another sip of brandy.

Her father studied Becky's tearstained face. "Becky, why are you so convinced that Miss Hendrix is innocent?"

It was a hard question.

"Because . . . because she didn't burn the music house. Because she couldn't have. Because she was hunting for starfish. And because—because her sister lied. Oh—just because I am!" She finished desperately. "Somehow I'm going to prove it. I'm going to hunt for the bracelet. I've got to."

"Charles?" her mother pleaded. "Aren't you going to stop her?"

Her father poured himself a little brandy.

Becky waited.

"No, Tilly, I don't think I am. But Becky . . ." He

went to her and held her chin in his hand.

"Yes, daddy?"

"Becky, it would be better for all of us, if you're right. You do know that, don't you?"

THAT NIGHT as she lay in bed and looked into infinity, Becky made up a riddle:

Riddle me, riddle me, riddle me ree. It's all as strange as it can be. Who is X? And who is Z? And what did the mermaid truly see?

ten

They dawdled over breakfast the next morning. No one had slept well the night before, and no one was eager to face the new day, in spite of Hank Forrester's prediction that it was going to be beautiful. Hank Forrester was the early morning radio weather man, and they regarded him as their one friend in Quoneck. When they heard his "Good morning, folks," they always responded with, "Good morning, Hank." They liked Hank; not only did he sound reliable, but as if he cared and tried hard to give them good weather. In Quoneck, weather was big news, not merely a question of whether or not to carry an umbrella. Here, you knew that the fishermen's livelihood could be cut off if the weather was bad—and here, you knew that, depending upon the weather, a fire could or could not be controlled.

A beautiful day. "A touch of spring at last," Hank had said, with a decided lilt to his voice. "Thanks, Hank," Becky had responded gloomily. That meant that this afternoon after school, Priscilla and some new I.C. would get Baskin-Robbins ice cream cones, would meander down to the Soldiers' and Sailors' Monument on Riverside Drive and, as they leaned over the balustrade facing the river, would imagine themselves to be on the balcony of their castle, waiting for their knights to return from a quest.

"Fink!" Becky muttered.

Her mother and father, deep in their own gloom, did not hear this.

"What are you going to do today, Becky?" her father asked, casually.

"Oh, I don't know. Read, maybe."

"All day?"

"Maybe."

"And tomorrow?" His voice was gentle.

"Read some more."

"Becky—I don't blame you one bit. But you can't hide from the kids of this village forever. I thought you were going to hunt for the bracelet."

"Charles! Why are you encouraging Becky to do something dangerous?"

"Who says its dangerous?" he asked.

"I do. The whole world's trying to get Johnny to read more, and here you are discouraging her, and sending her, your own child, off on a dangerous mission."

"Don't be ridiculous. It may be futile to try to uncover a little bracelet that was lost sixty-five years ago . . . but dangerous? Nonsense."

"Well, I don't like it and suppose—"

Becky broke in: "What's sixty-five years? On digs, they dig up stuff that's been buried for centuries."

"And suppose," her mother persisted, "you run into that Z person again? Isn't the ruin out on the marsh?"

Becky wished her mother hadn't reminded her of that.

"Oh," she said, with bravado, "now I'll get there by way of the Mermaid. Besides, he must be gone by now . . ."

Just then the phone rang.

"Oh-oh," Becky said, as she went to answer it. "Here we go creepy crawly again."

But it was Mr. Mills at last. He was off on business and wondered whether Becky was free to pick up Winky and keep her for the day? Becky forgot all about her desire to hide from the kids. Oh yes, she certainly was free.

"Waifs and strays, waifs and strays," her mother complained when she heard the news.

"Waifs and strays!" Becky protested. "Winky is a very aristocratic dog whose ancestors are all champions. She is classy and so is Mr. Mills. You're going to like them."

"Both of them?"

"Yes. He's nice and friendly, and Winky is adorable. And aren't you happy I'm going to make money?"

"Thrilled," her father said, with undisguised irony.

Becky waited to pick up Winky until after school had started; nevertheless, she still kept her eyes out for a laggard or a truant. She saw neither.

When she went through the gate of The Gull, she looked to see if Alfie Stone and "his mob" had thrown any beer bottles into the yard. If they had, they had been whisked away. Not a pebble, not a blade of grass was out of place here. Anyone who would throw a beer bottle into this yard had to be mad at Mrs. Bolton—or the whole world.

The doorbell was a large brass knob, and Becky had to fiddle with it before she discovered you pulled it out and pushed it back to make it ring. It rang with a lovely chime, which was followed by the sound of pattering feet, and the sound of a bolt being scraped. A bolted door in Quoneck? In the morning?

"Yes?"

The question descended from an exceedingly tall, exceedingly thin woman who fluttered nervously.

"Excuse me, is Mrs. Bolton here?" Becky asked.

"Of course I'm here. Where else would I be at this hour of the morning?"

"I—I'm the dog sitter and . . ."

"I know who you are. Come in, come in. What a morning, what a morning, one thing after another, phone hasn't stopped ringing, toilet overflowed, this village is all upset, Winky, Blinky, all too much. You're that new little girl, aren't you?" Without waiting for Becky to admit to it, she raced on, breathing noisily, "Follow me, follow me, I hope you know all about dogs, I'm a cat person myself; Blinky is a mighty expensive dog, Mr. Mills is a lovely person. Oh! Oh! Oh!"

Becky stumbled.

"I forgot to bolt the door. Locks, yes. But a bolt too? here in Quoneck? where I was born and raised and so were my ancestors? But I say better safe than sorry." When she came back from bolting the door, she bent down and stared hard at Becky. "This was a beautiful, quiet village to live in before . . . here we are." She stopped in front of a closed door. Hearing them, Winky became hysterical with joy.

"All right, Blinky, all right," Mrs. Bolton cooed, as she opened the door.

Becky crouched low and let Winky attack her with kisses and pawings and tiny nibbles, with a heart bursting with love.

"Lovely man, Mr. Mills. Thoughtful," Mrs. Bolton was rattling on, "quality always thoughtful. I'm a student of human nature. Leaves the place neat as a pin. I don't take in riffraff, you know. People have to be recommended. A recommendation from Carter Adams is good enough for me. Mr. Mills is one of those big, important lawyers, I am told. It's nice of him to be giving you a job, thoughtful. And he's courtly too. Quality is always courtly. In this business you get to know who's who and why. I imagine your parents made the acquaintance of Euphemia . . . in New York?"

"They didn't make her acquaintance anyplace. They never saw her in their whole lives."

Mrs. Bolton stuck her tongue in her cheek. "Well, well, well . . . fancy that . . ." She handed Becky Winky's lead and a small paper bag. "Blinky's treat. Food in the rooms is not usually permitted, but you can see for yourself that Mr. Mills is an exceptionally neat and clean gentleman. Makes all the difference in the world when you're neat and clean. Neat and clean is on the preferred list at The Gull and I make no bones about it."

Becky smoothed out her rumpled T shirt, then turned to Winky. She stood on her hind legs, pawing and hopping up and down, making it difficult to put her lead on. Mrs. Bolton fluttered nervously. "Are you sure you'll be able to manage her?" Becky didn't bother to answer that. When the lead was finally on, Winky pulled for the door.

"Just a minute," Mrs. Bolton ordered.

Becky braced herself.

"You can't blame them, our kids, I mean," she said. "You see, we all know what we know, because this is *our* place. No one appreciates outside agitators, that's a fact of life. And a friendly tip. Now, mind you take good care of Blinky. She's a pretty precious dog. Aren't you precious, precious?"

There were no secrets in Quoneck. The conviction sent an icicle up Becky's spine.

Becky spent most of that day cuddling Winky, trying to teach her to sit, and walking her where she was unlikely to meet anyone. Even her mother fell in love with Winky.

Late afternoon, when Mr. Mills picked Winky up, the siren went off again.

"Oh, no," Becky's mother moaned.

"How long has this been going on?" Mr. Mills asked.

Her parents didn't know.

". . . but too long for me," her mother said.

"I wouldn't like it either," Mr. Mills said, sympathetically. "Most particularly not in a village like this. However, I'm sure they'll catch the culprit before long. They usually do. I wonder where this fire is."

Becky's father fetched the chart. "This one is at the railroad station. I guess because it's daylight and no one is there, no trains coming through now."

"Did they try to keep it a secret from you too?" her mother asked, "the way they did us? Because we're outsiders?"

"Actually, no. Adams was outspoken about it. He's put on some extra security at night. He's got a pretty penny invested in that boat yard, you know."

"I can't see an old woman creeping around a boat yard at night," Becky's father said.

Becky thought she saw Mr. Mills look too intently at her father, slightly suspiciously.

"Oh, so you've heard about the suspect too. Of course, she could have an accomplice," Mr. Mills said, quietly. "Some dumb kid who needs a dollar."

"It doesn't make sense," her father said.

"That's the whole point," Mr. Mills agreed. "It doesn't. Very sad. Who knows what can set off a spark—if you'll forgive the pun—in a bitter, lonely, not quite rational old woman?"

"I—" Becky began.

Her father interrupted quickly. "Did Adams say anything to you about what evidence they have of arson? I mean some of these fires may be legitimate. This one at the station, for instance. A cigarette thrown from a passing train . . ."

"Exactly. This one may very well be legitimate. No, Adams didn't mention evidence. Where there is a suspicion of arson, any evidence is usually kept under wraps until the case comes to court. As for the hysteria, I find it understandable in a tightly packed village like this, although I am sure most of it is not warranted. After all, none of these fires have been a really dangerous threat."

"So far . . ." her mother said.

"So far," Mr. Mills agreed.

Mr. Mills thanked Becky for taking care of Winky, paid her five dollars, and assured her that he would call on her again on a future visit.

"You're leaving?" her father asked.

"Most reluctantly. Arson or not, I find this place appealing. Sadly, business does make demands.

However, when Adams turns up an attractive charter, I shall be back to check it out." He hesitated, then looking at the three of them, he said, "Everything takes time."

"Nice man," Becky's mother said, after he'd gone.

"Yes," her father said, but his thoughts were elsewhere. "Becky, I'd like to meet Miss Hendrix. Is that possible?"

"Gosh. I don't know. She's like a lady hermit. Why do you want to meet her?"

"Very simply, I don't like having you this involved. If these fires continue to happen . . . It's all very well for Mills to pooh-pooh them, he doesn't live here. I've decided I can't let you—and us too—be this isolated."

"Daddy!"

"Don't argue, Becky. I want to meet her. I want to decide for myself whether I think she's to be trusted. And, if I think she is, I might help."

"How?" Becky and her mother asked together.

"I don't know yet. Get the phone book, will you, Becky?"

"Daddy—I feel funny about this . . ."

"So do I," her mother said. "I hope you know what you're doing, Charles."

"You're an encouraging pair, I must say."

Miss Hendrix was not listed in the phone book. Miss Hendrix, Information said, had an unlisted number.

"Then we'll drive up there. Come on, Becky."

"Now?" her mother protested. "Before dinner? With night coming on? Have you lost your mind?"

"Quite the contrary. Hurry, Becky, before it gets dark. We'll be back soon."

"You'd better be!"

eleven

Nature was bringing a beautiful day to a beautiful and showy close as they drove off. The western sky was on fire with gold and crimson, and the eastern sky was serene with a rising moon and the evening star.

"Starlight, Starbright, first star I've seen tonight . . . I wish, I wish my wish comes true," Becky murmured.

Her father didn't ask what she had wished for, he just patted her knee.

With a great surge of longing, what she had wished for was for all their troubles to disappear— pronto!

"Why am I so dumb? Why can't I mind my own business?" she asked her father.

"Inherited weakness," he answered.

"Yeah, I know. You're being as dumb as I am. If

we have to move from here, where will we go?"

"I don't know."

The answer was a surprise. She had expected him to say: "Don't be crazy. Who's going to move?" This answer made her stomach drop with fear. He must be feeling hopeless, not just about this Hendrix business, but about not finding work.

"Moving could be good," she said, wistfully.

"Don't count on it, Becky."

"Who's counting?"

By the time they reached the Mermaid, the sun was only a narrow band of gold in the western sky. Her father pulled up at the entrance to the driveway and gazed at the house. The mermaid was pointed toward the sea; in the growing twilight, the house seemed animate and secretive . . . and waiting.

"Isn't it beautiful, Daddy?"

Her father whistled. "Yes," he said. "It is that. People have murdered for less."

"O-o-h!" Becky shuddered, half seriously.

"Go up and find out if she'll see me."

"Alone? Gee "

"It's more polite than having me barge in. Run along. She won't shoot you."

"Stop that!"

"I thought it would amuse you."

"It doesn't."

Becky didn't enjoy walking up the driveway. Suppose . . . ? she began and then ordered herself to stop supposing. She looked up and saw the star still twinkling away. If only it really could make her wish come true.

When she reached the front door, she looked back. A mistake. The Beetle seemed miles away and smaller than ever.

The house was too quiet and no light was to be seen in it at all. The knocker was brass and attached to a lion's head. She rapped it once, timidly. Nothing happened, and she rapped it again.

"What is it? Why have you come?"

Becky's knees buckled.

Miss Hendrix had come up behind her without making a sound. Why was she always sneaking up on people? And why was she so unfriendly?

"I . . . I . . . I . . ." Becky stammered.

Miss Hendrix waited.

"My father is down there." She pointed to the Beetle. "He would like it if you would see him. Please."

Miss Hendrix looked toward the Beetle, kept on looking.

"It is a strange time for calling." Her voice was dark with suspicion.

"He says maybe he can help."

"Help? You told him all about me?"

"Yes. I had to."

"Had to? Why?"

"Because . . . because now everyone hates me."

"Yes, of course. I warned you it was dangerous."

She fluttered her hands irritably. "I knew I shouldn't have talked so much. I really don't like people interfering in my affairs. Even with the best intentions, I'm sure. I've always kept to myself, and I prefer it that way. My dear, I now set you free. You have absolutely no more responsibility. Do thank your father for me. And tell the children it's perfectly safe for them to befriend you. Now, if you'll excuse me . . ." She put her hand on the door knob.

"Okay," Becky said. Relief poured over her like a warm shower, soothing her hurt feelings.

She had taken only a few quick steps when Miss Hendrix called out to her.

"I didn't mean to be so rude. Oh, that's not it . . . the truth is . . . I can't afford to be stupid. I . . . please tell your father to come up."

"Oh!" Becky couldn't hide her dismay. To have been so close to freedom! If Miss Hendrix detected her dismay, she chose to ignore it, and went into the house.

On the walk back down the driveway, a rustle in the trees sent Becky flying. No matter if it was only a cat or a racoon. With night coming on, all unidentified sounds were suspect and she reported it to her father. He left the Beetle where it was, and took his flashlight with him. As they walked up, he swept it over the trees. To Becky, the quiet was more ominous than the rustling.

"Someone's watching us," she whispered.

Her father didn't say anything, and she clutched his hand.

The meeting between Miss Hendrix and her father was strained, to say the least. They sized each other up with undisguised wariness and kept their conclusions to themselves. For once, Miss Hendrix was out of the turtleneck. She was wearing a heavy denim pullover, canvas pants, and the same gloves Becky had seen the first time they met. Becky knew she had been digging.

Becky found herself wishing that her father's rumpled old denim jacket wasn't missing a button. And promptly hated herself for minding.

They seemed to take forever getting to the reason for the visit. Her father told Miss Hendrix how much he admired the house. He wondered how old it was. Miss Hendrix said it was early eighteenth century. It had been built by a reclusive whaling master. With great taste, her father added, and soundly. With love, Miss Hendrix countered, rather coolly. But of course, her father said, gently. Becky wanted to give them each a good poke and yell: "Stop playacting! and trust each other, you dopes!"

At last her father said, "Becky thought we were being watched as we walked up your driveway, Miss Hendrix."

Miss Hendrix stiffened. "Is that an accusation or a warning? I'm confused."

"Neither," he said. "May I look through your telescope?"

Miss Hendrix frowned. "Why didn't you ask immediately?"

"I'm not as imaginative as my daughter. May I?"

"You may. And if you see anyone I hope you're a good shot, because I've got a twenty-two."

He looked back over his shoulder at Miss Hendrix with concern. With a sinking heart, Becky knew that he was thinking about Nina's train being shot at.

Becky trotted across the room with him.

He swivelled the telescope away from the village and toward the wood behind the driveway.

"Do you see anything?" Becky whispered.

"No," he answered, but he kept his eye glued to the lens.

Miss Hendrix had remained standing in the center of the room. She was pulling her gloves off slowly, finger by finger.

Her father whistled softly.

"Miss Hendrix, come here. Quickly."

"I told you, I told you." Becky was in a state of nervous excitement.

Her father stepped aside and, after removing her dark glasses, Miss Hendrix looked into the telescope.

"Ah . . . yes . . ." she muttered. "I see someone with a flashlight. Why!" she raised her voice. "That's Alfie Stone! How dare he! What's he doing on my property?"

"Yes, what?" her father asked.

"I intend to find out! And she took off with a long, angry stride, looking very strong. "I'm getting my gun!"

"Just a minute, Miss Hendrix. I'm not sure . . ."

"You may not be, but I am. I simply am not taking any more of this nonsense. That hoodlum is up to no good."

"That may be. But I'm not sure you ought to go after him. Not yet. And certainly not carrying a gun."

"Why not?"

"I'm playing a hunch. Besides, you'll not catch him . . . And who is Alfie Stone?"

"A stupid young hoodlum. Partially retarded, if you ask me."

"Hoodlum?"

"Oh, yes. He's always in trouble of some sort, you know, the usual pattern—vandalism, petty thievery, now I suppose drugs . . ."

". . . and planting gasoline soaked rags . . . ?"

Miss Hendrix rested a hand on the edge of a table.

"Of course. Becky told you. I hadn't thought of that. And killing little birds. He's working for my sister I'm sure. He would do anything for a dollar or two . . . throw suspicion on me, try to drive me over the edge . . . Oh yes, it begins to shape up . . ."

"Working for your sister? And—or for someone else?"

"What does that mean?"

"I understand you have not been told who the buyer is, isn't that so?"

"Yes, it is."

"Haven't you wondered why? Been at all curious?"

"No . . . I can't say I have. I've had too much else on my mind. The lawyer has said someone very rich, someone Hope met out west. What difference does it make to me who it is? Why should I care?"

Miss Hendrix waved a fragile hand back and forth in front of her face, as if she were brushing away cobwebs. She quite visibly was losing her sudden burst of strength.

"Do please speak plainly. You see, I've been concentrating so fiercely on my sister . . . my mind has gotten a little fuzzy I'm afraid."

"Do sit down, Miss Hendrix. Naturally, this is all very trying for you."

"Yes . . . very trying." She fumbled her way to a chair. "You are kind . . . and you are only a stranger."

"I have a fairly big stake in this, Miss Hendrix. It's not kindness that brought me here. It's self-interest. Becky is being ostracized, and we are new here. We are, so to speak, all outsiders together, aren't we?"

"I warned the child it was dangerous. You're free. Both of you. I don't want to add gratitude to my other problems."

"You asked me to speak plainly, and I aim to please." Her father smiled faintly. "There's no need for gratitude. It's too late for that. It would help a lot, though, if somehow we could get the village to think more kindly of us than it seems to now. My thought, Miss Hendrix, is that we ought to try to de-mystify the prospective buyer. We ought to find out who—or what—X stands for. How would this village feel about let's say—having a nuclear installation here?"

Miss Hendrix took a minute to rearrange her attitude and her thoughts; then she came close to smiling. "They'd loathe it. Most of them, that is."

"I suspected so. Or—for instance, off-shore drilling for oil?"

Miss Hendrix shuddered.

"Or—as has happened in a town down the line, would they care for an infestation of shady characters?"

"I do follow you now. But how can we possibly find out?"

"I haven't figured that out yet. And of course I can be wrong. It may turn out to be someone as harmless as an eccentric rich recluse—like the original owner of this house."

"No, I won't have that. Please let it be someone absolutely horrible—oh, please."

Her father smiled. "I'll do my best." He became serious. "Now, I didn't just dream up the question of the mysterious buyer out of nowhere. I remembered that Becky saw a man wandering on the marsh, near the remains of your music house. I'm wondering if he could have been your sister's lawyer. Do you know him?"

"I've met him. He came to badger me."

"Could you describe him?"

"Politely?"

"As accurately as possible."

"I loathed him. I happen to loathe people who dip their tongues in sugar to disguise the poison. Short, soft, and exists on a diet of carbohydrates. 'Now, Miss Hendrix'," she mimed, " 'believe me, your sister has only your welfare at heart . . . what if you fell and broke your hip, all alone here . . . ?' " She laughed harshly. "Why on earth would I do that? My welfare? I thought I would die laughing. He has gray hair. And a predatory nose. I also loathed his tie. It was sickly green and glaringly yellow and absolutely ugly and must have cost a mint. Only my sister would have a lawyer who wore a tie like that. Does he sound like your man?"

"No," Becky said. "Mine was dark and sort of skinny. And I call him the Z man. He also almost killed us."

Becky's father explained about Z licenses.

"That is interesting . . ." Miss Hendrix mused. "Rather a distance to come in a rented limousine . . . and to shuttle back and forth in it? And what, *what* was he doing on the marsh?"

"You see why I think it would be good to know."

"But how does one do that? I simply cannot get involved with hiring detectives, if that's what you have in mind."

"No, it isn't. I thought I might be able to make a first step. With your permission . . ."

"And what would that be?"

"Becky memorized Z's license. And she didn't exaggerate. He did come close to killing us. I happen to have a friend in the New York Police Department. If we find out which limousine service owns that car, we might also find out who hired it."

"I absolutely give you permission to do that." She shivered. "I confess I am now quite frightened. The whole business does begin to smell of power, evil power. Are you sure you want to get involved?"

"I'm no hero, Miss Hendrix, but I'm afraid there's no alternative."

He didn't look at Miss Hendrix; he looked at Becky.

Becky looked at her sneakers.

"I didn't know you knew any cops," was all she said.

"When you work on buildings in New York, you get to know them."

114

twelve

After Becky's father said that he was going to try to help Miss Hendrix, Becky's mother stopped talking in capital letters. In fact, she rarely talked at all. Although they did not discuss it, Becky and her father found this infinitely more disturbing than her hysteria. It was as if she had resigned herself to total disaster—and thought them stupid and reckless not to do so too. She quite deliberately did not unpack some cartons, and she refused to buy a new tea kettle.

They, however, had to resign themselves to waiting: the man in the police department was out of town.

Waiting did not suit Becky's temperament; it made her restless and uneasy.

Excursions to the ruin were the best distraction.

Becky had managed to persuade herself—and her mother—that with the police about to know the number of Z's license plate, she had less to fear from him. And, besides, Miss Hendrix had directed her to the private path that led from the main house to the ruin. Confessing that her back was older than she cared to admit, Miss Hendrix had decided to accept help.

The music house had been a good distance away, and the path wound in and out of some rolling meadows, a stand of pine, and around a cove. Miss Hendrix's mother had wanted to be alone with her music. On the way, one had glimpses of the sea and the marsh and always the flash of gliding gulls. For Becky, it was at once a beautiful walk and one that led back to a terrifying—and unresolved—past. With its view of the music house, what *had* the mermaid seen?

Becky dug and dug and dug. She thought her own back would break; she got blisters; she got bored; and she lost hope. Tons and tons of dirt and one tiny bracelet lost so many years ago? Her father had suggested that she divide the site into squares and go at it square by square. But how deep? she wanted to know. Well, he was no archeologist, but he thought perhaps about a foot would do.

She dug and dug and dug—taking time out only to gaze at the gulls, or clouds that were interesting shapes, or for imagining this and that. Sometimes she tried imagining herself about to dig up the ruins of a lost city, but somehow that always led to imagining a young Euphemia and Luke playing together here and making their music. Too often, this imagining burst into violent flames and left Becky feeling sick and overwhelmed with sadness.

Twice in her digging she turned up Indian arrowheads. And there were bitterly disappointing times when an object that might have been a crusted-over gold bracelet turned out to be a rusty nail, or a bolt, or part of a tin can.

And once, she had the feeling that she was being watched. With her heart racing, she made an elaborate pretense of being overdue someplace: she looked at her watch, gasped, dropped her shovel, and made a hasty retreat back up the path.

She didn't tell Miss Hendrix about this. Sometimes, as she passed the house on her way to or from digging, Miss Hendrix would call out for her to come in and give her a report: How was the digging going? Had her father heard anything? How long was it all going to take? How *long?* Miss Hendrix was beginning to whisper in capital letters. And there were other more alarming signs of strain. Alfie Stone had become an obsession. Miss Hendrix heard his presence in every snapping of a twig, in every squeak of a floor board. "Alfie? Alfie Stone is that you?" Becky heard her call out more than once. "I don't sleep any more," she told Becky, "and I don't care who knows it, but my twenty-two is right next to my bed."

In the middle of a sentence, she would forget what she was talking about. She didn't know where she put things. The house was becoming untidy—the vases were filled with dead flowers, dishes were piled in the sink.

And she burnt a pot of green beans.

"It can happen to anyone," Miss Hendrix said, "anyone."

Becky agreed. Sometimes, she told Miss Hendrix, it had happened to her mother—in New York. Here, her mother'd gotten nutty on the subject of fire.

"Yes, of course," Miss Hendrix said, coldly.

Becky dropped her eyes.

Two days later, when Becky went past the kitchen, she smelled something burning. And panicked.

"Miss Hendrix! Miss Hendrix!"

She burst into the kitchen.

The room was filled with smoke. Miss Hendrix was sitting quietly beside a table; her elbow rested on it so that the hand supported her head. It was the picture of peaceful repose. Except for some tears dribbling down the powder dry old cheeks.

"So—she is winning after all," she said, the whisper barely audible. She pointed to a frying pan, still smoking. "I heated the oil and went to answer the telephone. I have been thinking of having it disconnected. But for some reason, I can't do it. It was the lawyer, badgering me again. Fortunately, I kept my head. I didn't tell *him* I was setting the house on fire. I said . . . what *did* I say? I believe I said someone was at the door. Yes, that's what I said. It's a good sign that I kept my head, isn't it?"

Becky didn't respond quickly enough.

118

"It isn't a good sign?" Miss Hendrix asked, pathetically.

"Oh, yes, I'm sure it is."

But, in a way, this second kitchen fire was the beginning of the end. What followed seemed almost inevitable.

When Becky came home that day, her father was in the living room reading the local newspaper. This room, more than the others, showed her mother's resistance to settling in: the walls were still bare of pictures, none of the little objects—the bowls and vases and ashtrays—had been unpacked.

He was reading the help wanted columns and didn't hear her come in. His face was drawn and tired.

"Hi," Becky said.

He looked up slowly, forced a smile.

"And how's our little gold digger?"

"Okay. I guess."

"What's the problem?"

Becky told him about the second burning of a pot.

"Poor old lady . . ." He looked worried.

"Do you think maybe she's going real crazy and is what do you call people who can't help starting fires?"

"Pyromaniacs."

"What if maybe . . . ?"

"Let's not jump to conclusions. Look here, Becky, she doesn't have to be a pyromaniac to burn a couple of pots. But if it's all getting too much for her, it may be getting too much for us too."

"You're not going to give up before you've even heard from your cop friend, are you?" Becky asked in disbelief. "*Desert* Miss Hendrix?"

"I'll thank you to skip the heavy moral indignation act. It's just possible that she shouldn't be living alone in that house. I'll give Reynolds another couple of days, and if I don't hear from him, and Miss Hendrix continues to show signs of cracking up . . ." He shrugged.

"What'll you do?"

"That is the question. I don't know. Unfortunately, she doesn't appear to have any friends here—and neither do we—so there's no one to talk to about it. I'll have to think about it. In the meantime, I'd really rather you weren't going up there so much."

"But the bracelet—"

"Becky, digging for that bracelet—if it's there—is like digging for the impossible."

"But we can't desert her now, can we?"

Her father looked at her with a mixture of exasperation and affection.

"Becky, in the future, do us a favor and stick to four legged animals. But now promise me you won't do anything stupid."

"Like what?"

"How should I know? Playing the heavy heroine or something else stupid—something . . ."

"Dangerous?"

"Yes."

"Yikes!"

Becky agreed to try not to be stupid, but secretly she wondered how in this alien world, she, a stranger, was to know what was stupid and what wasn't.

MR. MILLS returned, and so did Nina, on the same day.

Becky had begun to write about watching two gulls chase a little tern away, but interesting as that was, watching Mr. Mills and Nina was more so. So she found herself writing: "What's going on? Mr. M. came right out and right to her face told Nina she was a beautiful girl. As if she didn't know it. But she acted like it was the biggest piece of news she ever heard. She's an actress all right. I had all I could do not to clap my hands at *that* performance. But our mother thought that Nina accepted a gracious compliment gracefully. Gawd! And when Mr. M. discovered that N. wanted to be an actress, he hinted that he knew a bunch of big shots who might help. Unless I'm nuts, which I don't think I am, Nina fell flat on her face in love with Mr. M. right then and there. If it's going to be one of those December & May marriages, it's okay with me because that way we'll have Winky in the family. And money. Who could ask for anything more?"

The best part, though, of Nina's being so interested in Mr. Mills was that she paid no attention to Becky's doings with Miss Hendrix. And her visit was a good distraction for their mother.

Nina had come up on a Thursday, and was due to go back on the earliest train out on Monday. Mr. Mills stopped by twice in that time: once, to leave Winky with Becky on Thursday night, and then to pick her up on Saturday.

It was a surprise when he knocked on the door on Sunday, with Winky on a leash. Becky thought that he and Nina exchanged special, flirty smiles before he became grave and came to the reason for the visit. Another fire.

This suspicious fire had been in the basement of the school. Fortunately, it was Sunday. But the *school?*

"And . . ." Mr. Mills was speaking quietly, clearly trying not to be over-dramatic and unduly alarming, "they found a clue."

A clue? Becky felt a twinge of fear. Mr. Mills seemed to speak directly to her, and her heart began to pound.

"They found a woman's glove nearby."

Becky sputtered: "S-s-so what? Millions of women wear gloves."

Nina spoke sharply. "Becky, don't get so excited. Let Mr. Mills talk."

"I will so get excited!" Her throat was beginning to tighten.

"Becky's right," Mr. Mills said. "There's no proof, absolute proof, that the glove belongs to Miss Hendrix. It's just that her ex-gardener made the identification. It's an old kid glove, once soft and elegant, French, once used for going places, and now used for rough work. Gardening." He paused. "Or shoveling."

Becky lost her color, and her father moved closer.

"What are they going to do?" he asked.

"I believe the fire warden is going up to call on her. Merely to ask if it is her glove."

"Is she likely to admit that it is?"

"She may not."

"And if she does?"

"That is not conclusive proof that she set the fire, but . . . considering her history she might—by this time—be persuaded to get professional help, that is, to admit herself to a nursing home."

"And if she won't?"

"In my judgment that would be unfortunate. As far as I can make out—my informant is Adams—these people don't want to persecute an old woman like her. However, when the safety of a whole village is at stake, pressure may have to be exerted."

"Such as?"

"Oh, I don't know—petitions perhaps, deprivation of services such as plumbers, electricians, snow plowing, all that sort of thing."

"That's not pressure, that's harassment, enough to drive a troubled old woman over the edge for sure." Her father's voice bristled with rising anger.

"I agree. I said it would be unfortunate, and I'm happy it's not my problem. But that's why I took the liberty of stopping by to warn you because I gather it's yours. I think you'll agree with me that if you continue to side with the poor old woman . . ."

"She didn't do it! She didn't do it!" Becky shouted.

They all stared at her—her father, her mother, Nina, and Mr. Mills—and she grabbed Winky and buried her face in Winky's fur.

She heard her father thank Mr. Mills for his thoughtfulness in warning them and then she heard Nina say, in her most disgustingly fake grown-up voice, "Becky—Mr. Mills is waiting for you to let go of Winky." Becky wanted to kill her.

After Mr. Mills left, no one said anything for a minute or two. Then, Nina said: "At least we have *one* friend in this village."

Becky spoke to her father. "What are we going to do?"

"Nothing, I fervently hope," her mother said, in a small, tight voice. "This is not for strangers like us. It's too serious. You heard what Mr. Mills said. They're not monsters in this village."

Becky's father picked a spoon up from the kitchen table and examined it closely.

"Becky, I guess we ought to go up and see what's doing at the Mermaid." He said it softly, tentatively. When her mother and Nina both made protesting noises, his tone changed and became firm. "It's the least we can do."

Becky and her father reached the Mermaid's

driveway just as the fire warden's station wagon was coming out.

There was plenty of room for the Beetle to pass; nevertheless, the warden stopped. Becky's father signaled his thanks, and kept on going. The warden and two strange men watched them, stony-faced.

Becky crouched low in the seat. "Yikes—what'll the warden think about us?"

"It's too late to worry about that," her father said. "But that delegation looks bad."

The mermaid was trembling in the wind, pointed toward the sea. Clouds floated low, drifting seaward, and shadows were in motion everywhere. There was such an air of restlessness at the Mermaid, that it was not surprising to find Miss Hendrix walking the terrace, back and forth, back and forth, the cape billowing behind her. With her head turned toward the sea, she looked widowed and forlorn. The wailing of the wind drowned their footsteps.

"Miss Hendrix—" Becky's father shouted.

She turned and seemed to be neither startled nor surprised.

"May we talk to you?"

She nodded, but kept on walking.

"Here?" he shouted, in protest.

The wind died and, as if on cue, Miss Hendrix began: "Once I heard a mermaid on a dolphin's back uttering . . . how does the rest go? I've forgotten,

125

but it ends 'to hear the sea-maid's music.' Luke and I used to make up sea-maid's music . . . "

She attempted to hum, her voice now truly like an ancient instrument's, rusty from disuse, then she stopped with a little cry. "I suppose you know what's happened."

"Yes," her father said.

The wind came up again.

"Let's go in," her father shouted. "We must talk."

She looked up at the mermaid, then out to sea. Then she smiled and beckoned for them to follow her.

The room was sadder and more neglected than ever. Dried flower petals had blown all over the floor.

"The infestation didn't even have the courtesy to telephone before coming. I might have dusted some. Do sit down. Would you care for some tea?"

Her father shook his head, but he sat down and Becky stood next to him, leaning on him.

Miss Hendrix did not sit down. She kept on walking.

" 'We don't mean you any harm, Miss Hendrix,' they said . . . just be courteous enough, Miss Hendrix, to do this village a favor and crawl off to a hole and *die*. It so happens, that for some peculiarly personal reasons I'm not quite ready to die. Not quite, thank you."

"Miss Hendrix . . ." her father began, gently.

Just then Becky spotted the glove lying on a table.

126

She tugged at her father's jacket and pointed to it. She felt him stiffen.

"Miss Hendrix," he said, "don't you have your own lawyer, someone to advise you?"

She swung around. "Why should I need a lawyer? I'm not the one who's done anything wrong. What if the glove does belong to me? Is it a crime to be careless? I left it at the music house. Anyone could have picked it up, any trespasser that is, and deliberately planted it at the school. I wonder if that mysterious X, the would-be buyer of the Mermaid, knows what she's up to."

"But isn't she in California?"

"Who knows where she is? You can travel faster than sound on a broomstick, you know." She laughed shrilly. "I told them I saw Alfie Stone prowling my woods and—"

"And?" Becky's father prodded.

"And, my dear sir, their prejudice is such, so certain are they that *I* am the wicked witch, the insane arsonist of Quoneck, that they actually scolded me for making rash accusations. 'Now, Miss Hendrix,' they said, cooing disgustingly, as if they were talking to an idiot, 'what would Alfie Stone be wanting with your glove? He may have picked up a trifle here and there that didn't belong to him—boys will be boys—but what would he want with one glove? That just doesn't make sense, Miss Hendrix.' And when I suggested that perhaps it was for the precise purpose of blaming the fire on me, what did they say to that, those good men and true?"

"Yes, what?" Her father asked, keenly interested.

"They said I oughtn't to start accusing a young boy who's been mending his ways, maybe setting him back on the wrong path. Besides, they said, arson just wasn't Alfie Stone's bag." Propelled by her outrage, the words had been coming strong and steadily. Now, she faltered: "And then—and then I said—'But it is mine?' "

She walked to the French doors, where the view of the sea was unobstructed, and opened one. A strong gust blew in, scattering the petals on the floor.

"But it is mine?" she repeated. "They didn't answer. Not one of them had the guts to answer. Oh, what am I going to do? Who is going to help me?"

It was as if she were waiting for the sea to answer.

Standing up straight, Becky too could see the sea. It was darkening and the surf was roiling up, sending up clouds of spray.

She leaned close to her father and whispered, "We're going to try, aren't we, Daddy?"

He didn't answer at once.

"Yes, we'll try," he said, but he sounded bone tired.

thirteen

The "accident" happened two days later. "It was bound to happen," everyone said, as if fate were the guilty one.

Nina had gone back to New York Monday morning, genuinely concerned that she was leaving her family surrounded by enemies. And Mr. Mills had flown up to Maine to look over a boat Mr. Adams hoped would suit him. He had left Winky with Becky.

Since the music house was too far away for walking a little dog on a lead, she could not dig for the bracelet, and the truth of it was that she was glad.

Since word of the glove had gotten around, the tension in the village could be felt as if it were a natural force, like the weather; as if, in spite of clear skies, a major storm was in the making. It drove people out of their houses, and they were to be seen huddled in small groups everywhere, whispering, always whispering. At nightfall, Becky's mother locked the front door and the back door for the first time since they had come to Quoneck.

"Why?" Becky asked.

"Why must I know why?" her mother answered. "Why can't I lock some doors to keep the night air out if I feel like it?"

"It's okay with me."

And it was. The way things were going, it felt good to be separated—and defended—from the village with a turn of a lock.

That evening, instead of reading in the living room as they usually did, they sat around the kitchen table. Cozier. Becky's father was rereading *Moby Dick*, which he did about once a year; her mother was reading that morning's *New York Times*; and Becky was working on a jigsaw puzzle that had too much sky.

Actually, all of them, Becky knew, were listening: listening for the fire siren; listening for the phone to ring. (Either for a call from Reynolds, the New York policeman, or from the anonymous caller, who hadn't phoned in some time.) But mostly listening for any sounds that would unhappily justify their uneasiness.

After a while, Becky's mother ripped into their uneasy quiet. "I see that some poor blacks have gotten it again. The house they just moved into was set on fire."

Her father looked up from *Moby Dick*. "Don't be ridiculous, Mathilda," he said, sharply.

Becky looked up from a bewildering assortment of pale blue pieces. "Gee, you don't think—?"

"I said don't be ridiculous," her father said, still more sharply.

Her mother went back to the paper. "Poor people . . . it's so horrible . . ."

"Becky," her father said, "let's take Winky for a little walk . . . and a little ride."

"Kindly make it real little. I don't particularly feel like being here all alone."

They walked Winky up and down the dark and deserted street. Becky had not yet gotten used to the darkness of the village at night and the desertion.

Her father headed for the Beetle.

"Where are we going?" Becky asked.

"I thought we might knock on Miss Hendrix's door and see how she's doing."

"Oh." With Winky curled up on her lap, Becky slouched low in her seat. "They wouldn't sort of—you know—burn our house down, would they?"

"Of course not. Look here, Becky . . ." He didn't go on.

"Look here what?"

"Oh, I was going to make some kind of fancy speech, but I changed my mind. You don't want to hear any fancy speeches, do you?"

"No. Um—Daddy?"

"Yes?"

"Daddy, what'll we do if we never ever have any friends here?"

"It's not what *we'll* do, it's what will Quoneck do without us—charming, delightful, intelligent people that we are? Concentrate on that."

"Be serious."

"No. Let's not."

"But are you mad at me for getting us into this mess?"

"Not . . . quite . . . yet . . ."

"Daddy—I sort of feel like crying."

"Please, sort of control yourself."

"I'll try. Daddy, can people really be driven crazy?"

"Given certain circumstances, I imagine it's possible."

"Do you think maybe her sister made up this X buyer?"

"Why would she do that?"

"To drive her sister crazy and then she has the Mermaid all to herself?"

"Doesn't make sense to me."

"Who do you think shot at the train? And why?"

"I'm beginning to think I should have encouraged you to cry. Why don't you stop worrying so much?"

"I'm not worrying. I'm trying to figure things out. So—who do you think shot at the train?"

"I can't see Miss Hendrix doing that, if that's what's worrying you. Why would she?"

"If she's crazy she might. Crazy people do crazy

things. That's what crazy's all about."

Her father reached over and patted her knee.

"Becky—if you're preparing yourself for our side losing, I think that's wise."

Becky crouched still lower in the seat. Winky woke up and licked her ear.

It was a dark night, and the Mermaid was dark too. But when the Beetle's headlights picked out the driveway and started up it, a powerful outdoor light was turned on and off.

"What does that mean?" Becky asked, frightened.

"I don't know."

"Is what we're doing safe?" she whispered.

"Do be quiet."

As they drew up to the house, their headlights swept past the darkened lower windows of the Mermaid, past some budding shrubs and low, wind-twisted pines, until they blinded Miss Hendrix.

Becky's father stopped the car, but left the motor running.

Miss Hendrix was standing in front of the door with the twenty-two cradled in her arms, cradled like a malevolent baby.

"You stay here with Winky," her father ordered.

Becky watched as her father walked slowly toward Miss Hendrix, watched as Miss Hendrix shifted the rifle in her arms, watched as her father held out his hands. It was when Miss Hendrix handed her father the gun, that she realized that she had dug her nails into her hands.

Watching them talk to each other as they were caught in the beam of the headlights was like watching a puppet show without a narrator. Miss Hendrix kept running her fingers through her short hair till it was pulled out into a halo of wisps. Standing stiffly erect with the gun in his arm, her father looked like a sentry on the alert. Suddenly, they both turned toward the house, and her father, still holding the rifle, ran through the door with Miss Hendrix following as quickly as she could.

Without knowing what she was going to do—or why—Becky opened the door of the car. Beyond the wedge of light that the headlights made, it was a totally black world, the habitat of nightmares and their creatures. But if her father . . . she dared not finish the thought. Still clinging to the door, she stepped out of the car. She had not noticed that a light had gone on in the house until she saw her father move across a window. She closed the door quietly, whispered a word to Winky to stay still, and fled to the house.

Just as she got there, her father came out and grabbed her.

"Hey! I told you to stay put," he said.

"What's going on?"

"Go back to the car and wait. I'll be out in a minute."

"Why can't I come in?"

134

"Because Miss Hendrix doesn't need an audience."

"I'd rather wait here."

"Okay."

She sat down on the doorstep and drew her knees up close to her. Audience? For what? She tried to hear what was going on inside the house. All she could hear was the rhythmic sighing of a calm sea and the ominous silence of the surrounding blackness. Even the gulls were still. Once a twig snapped—or was it some pebbles shifting? Was it? Her heart raced, and she stood up and grabbed the door knob.

It turned in her hand, and her father opened the door.

"Now what?" he asked, low.

"Sh-h-h!" she cautioned. "Someone may be out there."

Her father stood still, listening. She had expected him to tell her she was silly, too imaginative, or too easily scared. That he did not do this, frightened her more than ever.

"All right, here we go," he said, in an abnormally loud voice. "I'll take you home, and then we'll come back."

"Who's we?" she whispered, as they walked to the Beetle.

"We'll talk in the car," he whispered back.

Instead of turning the car around, as he would

ordinarily have done, he backed and filled several
times trying to illuminate as much of the blackness
as possible. If anyone was lurking there, that
person—or persons—was well hidden.

They drove down the driveway slowly and
through the gate. Her father got out and secured it
carefully. Becky stuck her head out the window and
looked back at the Mermaid. Once again, it was
dark.

"Are you really going back?" she asked her father
as they drove off.

"I offered to, but she wouldn't have it. I also asked
her to come back with us, but she wouldn't do that
either."

"But what's going on? Tell me."

"Harassment. Ugly, stupid harassment. Telephone calls, one after another, some threatening."

"I thought her phone was unlisted."

"In a village like this it doesn't necessarily stay
unlisted."

"Is that why you ran into the house the way you
did, as if a murderer was there?"

"Yes. I wanted to answer myself."

"What did you say?"

"Oh, whatever came to mind that I thought might
appeal to their decency. Poor Miss Hendrix. Cow-
ardly way to behave . . . veiled threats to call in the
state police . . . but I soon realized that I was talking
to dead air. I told her to keep the receiver off the

hook, only to use the phone to call me if she needed me. I persuaded her to try to get some sleep."

"If it's only telephone calls that were going on, why couldn't I come in?"

"She didn't want a child to see an old woman weeping the way she was. She's a proud woman."

"Is she—safe all alone there?"

"I'm not going to kid you, Becky. I'm sure she's *physically* safe. I truly don't believe they are monsters, the people of this village. Yes, I do think I believe that. Unless . . . one or two are . . . But they're frightened. And some of them are probably stupid and insensitive. And I don't know how much more she can take—without cracking."

"Why can't you stop them, Daddy?"

"Becky, it's about time you knew that I'm not the all powerful being I used to be when you were younger."

"I sure wish I'd find that bracelet."

"I don't know how much good that would do now."

"It would prove that her sister lied about the bracelet because *she* was the one who set the fire, not Miss Hendrix . . . and . . . and . . . Miss Hendrix would feel better, not all crazy in the head . . ."

". . . and everyone would get to love her, and so it would follow that they would get to love us too and . . . Becky, my dear daughter, don't count on it."

But she did count on finding the bracelet. How else was she going to vindicate herself with the kids in the village?

They had not driven very far when they saw a police car cruising slowly. And farther on, where the dirt road to the Mermaid met the blacktop, some flashlights. Her father saw that the three men who held them were volunteer firemen.

"I guess they've organized a bit of a watch tonight," her father said.

"You mean they're spying on Miss Hendrix? Can they do that?"

"Why not? They're not on her property."

"They better not be. What did you do with her gun?"

"It was empty, and I didn't see any ammunition around. Frankly, even if she wanted to, I don't think she'd have the strength to shoot anyone tonight."

"How did you get it away from her out there?"

"With my usual gallantry. I bowed and said, 'Madam, allow me—that ain't a fittin' object for a lady to load herself down with—' "

"Seriously."

"Seriously, I just said let me hold that for you. And she did. Simple as that."

"Do you think she knew it was empty?"

"I hope so."

THE AFTERNOON papers came in to the village at four o'clock and that's when it happened. The

138

police record read 4:13. It was that precise because Officer Norman Grant was having his coffee break in Jack's Place when he heard the crash—and the scream—and, being a conscientious man, he looked at the clock and made a mental note of the time.

Tuesday was a beautiful afternoon with excellent visibility, exactly as Hank Forrester had predicted, which made it seem more than ever deliberate, rather than accidental.

Although four o'clock was the time that the kids of Quoneck would be wandering around—in and out of Trento's, or the Community Center, or each other's houses, Becky had had no choice but to take Winky for a walk. Winky had made it clear that she needed to be walked, and her mother had said she needed milk for New England clam chowder. (Since it had been chowder that had brought them to Quoneck in the first place, her mother thought it was high time she tried her hand at it. Maybe, she had said, this time it would act in reverse and get them out.)

The village was at its prettiest that afternoon. Lilac and apple and cherry were beginning to blossom and were scenting the air. Swans sailed through clear blue water, and gulls glided serenely overhead.

Becky had walked Winky in and out of the streets, pausing to study nature, which she had been neglecting. It was when she was bending over to study a chipmunk carrying a leaf home that she heard the crash—and the scream.

139

She picked Winky up in her arms and ran to Main Street, where the sounds had come from.

On Main Street, people were leaving the shops and heading toward a small cluster of people gathered in the middle of the street. Some kids were also running toward it.

Forgetting her enemies, Becky had to go too.

The car was up on the curb; its front was pushed up against a lamppost; some fluid was pouring out of its motor; and glass littered the road. A mangled bike lay mute and eloquent out in the road.

Becky saw Officer Grant and several people leaning over someone lying on the sidewalk.

There were some who might have been surprised at the strange quietness of this street scene, but Becky, who had witnessed similar scenes, was not. Unless there was some screaming, it was not until the police cars and the ambulances came along that the terrible noise usually began.

And then she saw Miss Hendrix.

Miss Hendrix was half sitting, half lying on the stoop of the Quoneck Dry Goods Store. Her glasses were crooked, and one eye was exposed. Her mouth was stretched in a ghastly grimace.

Becky pushed her way through until she reached her. She still held Winky in her arms.

"Miss Hendrix . . ." It was louder than she meant it to be in this quiet.

Miss Hendrix gave no sign of seeing or hearing

her. Her head was twisted to one side; with her aquiline nose and cropped hair and with the cape spread out, she looked like a wounded eagle that had plummeted to earth.

"Miss Hendrix, it's me, Becky. What happened?"

"She hit Alfie Stone, that's what happened," someone said, in a voice cold with anger.

Miss Hendrix's twisted head jerked back, as if it had received a blow.

Alfie Stone? She's *killed* him!

Becky felt a hand on her shoulder and looked up to see her father standing beside her. His face was gray.

"Did she kill him?" Becky whispered.

He didn't answer and sat down beside Miss Hendrix. He took her hand in his and began to chafe it, but she didn't respond to him either.

Officer Grant moved slowly through the small crowd, and he too went up to Miss Hendrix.

With one foot on the stoop, he leaned over and said, gently, "Miss Hendrix . . . you hurt anyplace?"

With her head still averted, she moved it slightly to indicate she wasn't hurt.

"Miss Hendrix," he went on, "Alfie says you saw him entering Main Street. He says you were looking right at him."

Her head remained still.

Becky's father spoke: "Officer, Miss Hendrix may

be in shock. Isn't there a doctor . . . ?"

"Thomas is out of the village today," the officer said.

"What about the boy? Doesn't he need a doctor too?"

"May have a shoulder out. That's all. He'll get himself x-rayed. Young and spry's what saved him."

"Norman . . . ?" A pretty young woman in a blue visiting nurse's uniform came forward. "What about my looking Miss Hendrix over? See if there are any possible fractures?"

"Yeah. Thanks, Pat. Didn't know whether to call the ambulance."

Miss Hendrix brought her head around and straightened her glasses. She addressed the nurse in a whisper that just barely carried: "I always said I wouldn't break any bones, and I didn't."

"Yes, dear," the nurse said, but went over her quickly and expertly. She spoke to the officer. "I think she's right. Nothing seems to be fractured. But she's cold as ice. I've got some brandy in my bag in the car."

Officer Grant took his book out of his back pocket and turned to the group. Curiously, it had stepped back, away from Miss Hendrix and Becky and her father, making them seem isolated. "Any witnesses?" he asked.

No one spoke up.

Becky's arms were aching from holding Winky, and she put her down.

"No one saw Miss Hendrix hit Alfie?" the officer asked.

Still no one spoke up.

"Who screamed?"

A large, red-faced woman said, "I did, Norman."

"Well, Mary, then you were a witness to the accident, right?"

"I wouldn't want to say I actually saw it happen. I saw Alfie on the bike all right, and I saw Miss Hendrix in her car, but I can't say that I actually, with my own eyes, saw her hit Alfie. I can't say that. I saw the result. And then, yes, I screamed. You all know I'm not one of your screamers by nature; but like a lot of other people in this village, I haven't had a wink of sleep in three nights. I'm a wreck, pure and simple. Norman—they're going to take her license away anyway, aren't they? I mean, we all know she's got two strikes against her—one for speeding once and one for going past a stop sign on Pine Hill road. That means this is it for her, doesn't it? Besides—the car is totaled too, isn't it?" She turned to the crowd of quiet people. "Don't we all want to just let her go in peace? Without us having to be witnesses and all that jazz?"

"Mary, she's entitled to her day in court."

"But where's she going to be in the meantime?" another woman asked.

"She needs to be in a hospital," the woman called Mary said.

"And we need for her to be there too." someone

else in the crowd said.

"She needs to be in jail."

Becky and the others turned, and Becky saw Alfie Stone with his arm slung in a bandana.

"Yeah," he said, "she saw me all right, and she came right at me. She's a menace, that's what. And look at my bike. That bike cost me a hundred bucks. If I hadn't-a jumped like a cat I'd be dead. None of us is safe with her loose."

"She's not going to be loose, Alfie," Officer Grant said, coldly. "But you know of any special reason for her going after you in particular?"

Becky held her breath.

"Yeah," Alfie drawled. "Like maybe she saw me trying to be some kind of a hero, trying to catch her setting one of them fires." He grinned at the crowd. "Yeah, I admit I trespassed once, or coulda been twice . . ."

"Okay, Alfie, that's enough. This isn't a court of law. Once more, any witnesses?"

Miss Hendrix placed her hands on the stoop and, leaning on Becky's father, she managed to stand up. Her thin body wobbled so much that if Becky's father hadn't quickly grabbed her, she would have toppled over.

"I . . . I . . ." her cracked whisper carried well this time, ". . . I am the witness. I seem to have done it . . . done it. I am terribly tired. And you are all rude to speak of me . . . as if I were an . . .

inanimate object. Unspeakably rude. Please, someone be kind enough to take me home to the Mermaid."

Her teeth were chattering.

The nurse came back carrying a flask and began to open it. Miss Hendrix waved it away. "Get me to your car."

"Norman," the nurse asked, "what about my taking Miss Hendrix to the Mermaid and staying with her overnight? Hospital's all filled up, you know."

"Well, I'll check headquarters on that, Pat."

Becky's father put his arm around Miss Hendrix and, with the nurse on the other side of her, they led her away. The crowd made a path for them, and Becky stuck close by. She was squeezing back tears and looking at the ground. But when she saw Clarissa and Van and Peggy, she stopped and said: "She didn't do it. She didn't do it. I know she didn't."

They just looked very solemn and didn't say a word back to her.

Miss Hendrix, now trembling from head to foot, was stretched out on the back seat of Pat's car with a blanket over her when Officer Grant returned. Pat waited for him out on the street, out of earshot of Miss Hendrix.

"They seem to think it's okay, Pat. You'll stay the night with her?"

"I said I would."

"And keep an eye on her? You know what I mean?"

Pat frowned. "Norman, don't be dumb. She's a wreck. I'm going to put in a call for one of the doctors from the hospital to come up there and look her over."

"Should I follow you up?" Becky's father asked.

Pat hesitated.

"She knows us. She knows we are her friends." He said this so that everyone standing around could hear.

"Well—it might be a good idea at that," Pat said.

Following her father to the Beetle, Becky stole a glance around. The crowd had broken into small clumps. Still quiet, they were all looking at her father and her.

Becky picked Winky up and got into the car.

"Becky," her father said, as he turned the motor on, "I told you to prepare for defeat."

"Well, I'm not."

"Not what? Not prepared? Not defeated?"

"She didn't do it. She didn't do it. I don't care what anyone says."

"Including herself?"

"I know all about bikes, you know. Anyone who's any good can jump off a bike and *shove* it in front of a car and make it look like it was hit. I saw a kid in New York do that. Only that time the driver wasn't an old lady, it was an off-duty cop and that kid was in real trouble."

"Becky, it doesn't matter anymore. She's lost the Mermaid. Accept it. Accepting defeat is part of growing up."

"I won't accept it. Besides, I'm too young to grow up." She stifled a sob.

"You have a point there."

"Daddy, she looks so awful. Do you think she's going to die?"

"No. She may want to, but dying isn't easy either. Of course, we don't know anything about her health . . . her heart . . ."

"Well, if Miss Hendrix dies, someone's committed murder."

Becky's father turned his head sharply toward her, then back to the road.

"Do you think that cop friend of yours is ever going to call?"

"Becky, I repeat: it doesn't really matter anymore. Whoever it is who wants to buy the Mermaid has got it. The sister will not have much trouble now being declared the conservator—or whatever—and then she can sell it to X or Y or Z or anyone else."

"But suppose it's what you said—X is an off-shore oil driller or a nuclear thing or something else awful? Won't the village get mad?"

"That'll be their problem."

"Daddy! Are—are you giving up?"

"I'm thinking of it."

"You mean we may go back to New York?" Becky didn't try to hide her excitement.

"New York's probably out. Let's not talk about it now, okay?"

It wasn't okay, but she said it was. If it wasn't going to be New York, then where? Were they going to keep on going from village to village and be outsiders forever?

The Mermaid too seemed more beautiful than ever that afternoon. The meadows were rippling in a gentle breeze. Lilac and fruit trees were beginning to bloom there too. Some plovers were feeding on the terrace. Startled, they took off on their dainty, racing little legs and flew toward the sea. But Becky knew they'd keep on coming back until Miss Hendrix was gone.

Becky left Winky in the car and watched her father and Pat get Miss Hendrix into the house, where they set her down on the chaise in the living room.

"I've given her some brandy," Pat said. "Now I'll try some tea."

"Is she bad?" Becky whispered.

"She's badly shook up, poor old thing," Pat answered.

"Old woman," Becky corrected.

Her father followed Pat into the kitchen.

Miss Hendrix was lying there with her eyes closed. The window was open and the breeze blew a strand of white hair across her forehead. Becky brushed it away and took Miss Hendrix's hand in hers. It was so ice cold it sent a shiver through Becky.

"Miss Hendrix." she whispered close to her ear. "Don't worry."

Miss Hendrix opened her eyes slowly, as if the lids weighed a ton.

"I'm home," she whispered.

"Yes, yes you are."

"Thank you." She closed her eyes again and sighed softly, peacefully.

fourteen

As the visiting nurse had gone about her nursing duties—which meant rummaging through cupboards and bureau drawers, poking into corners, even tidying up—the Mermaid already seemed lost to Miss Hendrix.

"And yet," her father said, as if reading Becky's mind, ". . . at least one feels that here she *had* heard mermaids singing—which is more than most of us have." They were standing next to the Beetle, looking back at the house.

And now they're crying, Becky thought.

The village had cleaned up after its unpleasantness. The car had been hauled away, the glass had been swept up, only a smear of oil remained as evidence. The villagers had broken their silence. Those who had lingered were now at their ease. Talking to each other, leaning against bikes or cars or the fronts of buildings, they were no longer stiff with tension.

As the Beetle went slowly down Main Street, some heads glanced at it and abruptly turned away. The people of Quoneck were not rubberneckers.

"I didn't get the milk for Mommy's clam chowder," Becky said low, as if the people on the streets could hear her.

"I don't know about you, but I don't have an appetite for New England clam chowder tonight."

Apparently, neither did her mother, because when they walked into the kitchen they smelled a chicken gumbo.

"I heard the news on the radio," her mother said, stirring the soup. "How is she?"

"Resting," her father said.

"What did they say on the radio?" Becky wanted to know.

"That she hit a boy on a bike, that no major injuries appear to have been sustained, and that the car was totaled. Then there was some editorial comment about this being her third offense—if found guilty, of course. Does that mean her license is going to be suspended, Charles?"

"I suppose so."

"It's the end of the road for her then, isn't it? I mean she can't live there without a car, can she?"

"Hardly."

Her mother looked back over her shoulder at

Becky. "Becky—honey, I'm truly sorry it turned out this way."

Then she let out a little yelp.

"Charles, I almost forgot to tell you. Your cop friend called. He said you could call him back. He'll be there until seven. But it doesn't matter much any more, does it, who this Z man is?"

Her father shrugged.

"Yes it does," Becky said. "*I* want to know who he is. *I* love the Mermaid. And I don't want anyone awful to get it. Or—or to knock it down for some rotten nuclear something . . ." Her voice was trembling.

"Calm down. I'm calling back because it's polite and because I'm curious. But as for making the preservation of the Mermaid my life's work, don't count on it, Becky." He went to the upstairs phone.

Becky headed for the cupboard where the Fig Newtons were kept.

"Uh-uh," her mother said, "not before supper."

The supper did smell good, so Becky didn't argue.

"How come you changed your mind about New England chowder so suddenly?" she asked.

"Oh, after I heard that news item, I thought that what this family could use tonight was some old-fashioned *southern* comfort. Get it?"

"I get it."

Her father came from the phone looking mildly surprised.

"Reynolds was very curious too about the Z man.

He's going to look into it immediately. Check out the license number and that sort of thing. He wondered what someone like that was doing out on a marsh so far from home."

"Will he call back?" Becky asked.

"Yes, he said he would. As soon as he has any information."

"How long will that take?" Becky asked.

"I haven't the faintest idea."

"Did you tell him how he almost killed us?" her mother asked.

"I did."

"And?"

"And nothing."

"*Nothing?* For all anyone knows, it could have been a deliberate attempt at murder."

Becky's father raised his eyebrows.

But Becky opened her eyes wide: "Mommy—are you serious?"

"Don't be ridiculous! Both of you!" her father snapped.

In bed that night, Becky tossed restlessly. Her brain was on fire thinking about Miss Hendrix, the Mermaid, the secrets, the X person, the Z man—and murder. It was a long time before she fell asleep, but somehow, by morning, the jumble had resolved itself into one single thought—the bracelet.

Hank Forrester was highly enthusiastic about the day ahead: it was going to be superb, he said, with good, clean air blowing in from the north. Winds up to twenty to twenty-five knots an hour, however, meant that a small craft warning was in effect.

A perfect day for digging. Becky's parents mumbled their usual discouragement, but her father agreed to keep an eye on Winky while he caught up with some correspondence. Becky knew he was running out of places to job hunt in the area and wondered if the correspondence had to do with jobs in far away places; the farther the better, she thought. Africa, for instance.

For lunch, she collected a chicken leg, two peanut butter sandwiches, an apple, and three Fig Newtons, and stuffed them into a bag. Today, there would be no diary, no nature books: it was to be all dig.

"Are you going to find out how Miss Hendrix is?" she asked her father just before she left.

"Aren't you going past the Mermaid on your way to your dig?"

"No. I want to take the long way. You call."

She didn't know why, but she didn't want Miss Hendrix to know about this dig.

"I'll call later," her father agreed.

"Do you think you'll know about the Z man by the time I come home?"

"Maybe yes, maybe no."

Winky, of course, knew she was going off and made a great fuss about wanting to go too. Becky squatted next to her and assured Winky that life without her, Becky, would be endurable for a few hours, that she was not being left with monsters, and that in any case, she, Becky, would return in the nick of time to save her.

"I'll be back, my darling Winky," she called out as she left. "Don't worry, I'll be back."

The village had returned to its own early morning quiet, secretive self. There had been no fire alarms during the night, the prime suspect was under house guard, and Quoneckers had caught up on their sleep.

The big fat black cat still did not accept Becky, still blocked her path.

"Ah, who needs you!" Becky snarled at the cat. She pedaled quickly through the village. Mrs. Bolton was out front sweeping her sidewalk, sweeping as if dirt was the enemy of all time. "Makes all the difference in the world when you're neat and clean."

"Sez you," Becky muttered under her breath as she arranged a smile with which to greet Mrs. Bolton. If Mrs. Bolton saw a girl on a bike wheeling past her, she gave no notice. "Ah well," Becky thought philosophically, "when they give me the Nobel prize for my research on fleabane, poor old Mrs. Bolton will regret this snub, old dumbhead that she is."

The rest of the trip to the marsh was made without meeting another soul. To be alone so early in the morning with nature was heady stuff, making her feel cocky and superior to all the poor drags who were just having their breakfasts and were getting ready for school.

At the marsh she left her bike behind and set out on foot. When she came to the bend, where she could see the Mermaid off in the distance, she stopped. "No! No! No!" she shouted and didn't care who heard her. "Nothing bad must happen to the Mermaid!" A gull answered with a squawk, some small birds broke from cover, and there was some fretting in the brush.

Up at the dig, Becky set her bag down on a pile of stones that had tumbled from the fireplace. A tiny green snake with yellow stripes slithered out. Becky stepped back, out of respect, she told herself, and studied it. From her scant study of snakes, she judged this one to be a harmless garter snake and let it go on its way with her blessings. She was quite pleased with herself for keeping her cool.

Before starting to dig, Becky looked around to see what spring had done to the ruin. Miss Hendrix had once pointed out the hawthorne and the lilacs and the roses that had mysteriously and miraculously survived the holocaust. They had been her mother's pets, she had said, and over the years she had tended them, feeding them and pruning them from time to time. That is, when she was grown up; as a child, she had never been able to go back there. Sometimes, she had said, it was her fancy that the hawthorne was Luke's spirit, the lilac her mother's, and that the roses would one day be hers.

Only the lilacs were budding.

The square Becky had been working on looked exceptionally small this morning, and the area still to be dug enormous. Her father was right; it was hopeless. If only she had been smart enough to try to win some of the kids over to her side, she could have organized a real dig. It was too late for that now; she'd have to do it herself, because only she knew how much finding the bracelet would mean to Miss Hendrix.

She began to dig. One or two dry days and the earth had already begun to harden. Becky pushed the shovel in as far as she could make it go with the full thrust of her arms, then she gave it an extra shove with one foot. "At least," she thought, "if nothing else, I've gotten to be a pretty good digger." She poured the shovelful of dirt slowly enough to examine it. Shovel after shovel of dirt yielded nothing more interesting than some ancient rusty nails and some ordinary small stones. Not even a worm or a slug or a spider for a naturalist to examine. As she continued to dig, Becky paused now and then. Once, it was to watch a tiny kingbird do battle with a hawk; another time, she watched a crow being chased from a nest by a pair of blackbird parents.

She must have dug for an hour or so before she decided she had earned a rest and *one* Fig Newton. Not a crumb more, she told herself sternly.

The rising sun had warmed the ruin of the fireplace, making it an inviting place to rest. But before picking a spot to lean against, Becky remembered the little snake and poked around to make sure it had no relatives who would come slithering out.

The fireplace had been made of flagstones and the chimney of bricks. Most of them had tumbled down over the years and lay scattered around the main foundation.

Satisfied that there were no more garter snakes in hiding, Becky found a spot where she could stretch out.

She munched very slowly on the Fig Newton to make it last as long as possible. When she had finished it, she was not quite ready to go back to dig. She began to fool around with some bricks and, as if they were playing blocks, she began to build a tower.

Arranging and balancing the bricks was an absorbing game, and she became choosy about the ones she would use. Only those that had been aged to a lovely pale pink suited her. Her roving eye caught a glimpse of one she wanted. It was partially covered with dirt and leaves and a rather large flagstone. She heaved the stone to one side and brushed the leaves and dirt away, then tried to lift the brick. It would not budge. She fetched the shovel to help dig it out of the hardened earth. At last, it was loosened.

She was pounding the brick on the ground to release the damp soil that clung to it, when she saw what looked like an earth encrusted ring. Certain that it was nothing but the remains of a tin can, she picked it up anyway. Wary of cutting herself, she cleaned it off as best she could. Suddenly, her heart began to knock against her ribs. This was no tin can. Blackened, and its hinge sticking, what she held in her hand was unmistakably a bracelet.

Wild with excitement, Becky forgot her lunch bag, forgot everything but the bracelet, and started to run toward the path to the Mermaid. Unhappily, she did remember her bike. She cursed herself for having come the long way, and began the descent down the slope, slipping and sliding in her haste, and clutching the bracelet for all she was worth.

At the bottom, she ran toward her bike.

Alfie Stone was waiting for her. His arm was not in a sling.

"Watcha hurry, kiddo?"

Even if she had had the breath, Becky knew she couldn't have spoken. She made a meaningless gesture with her free hand and made for her bike.

Alfie Stone blocked her path.

"Watcha got there in your hand?"

"Nothing."

"Let's see nothing."

He made a grab for the bracelet. Becky ducked and ran off the path and into the brush and wood, back up the slope. Wild with fear, she pushed branches and twigs back as she tried to run. Thorns caught at her. She stumbled and fell. She heard Alfie coming after her, heard him coming without calling out to her, coming in an evil silence.

She knew that he would catch her unless she could outwit him. If she could only get to the marsh without his knowing, and hide in the rushes and high grasses.

Stealthily, she began to backtrack in a semicircle. She could hear him thrashing about now. And then, because she had explored this part well, she found a place where she could make a leap into the marsh.

But she must land like a cat. She said a prayer and made the leap.

She didn't exactly land like a cat, but Alfie's own thrashing noises may have drowned the sound of her plop into the water. She pulled herself up on to a moist hummock and curled into a ball, saying another prayer.

The thrashing noises became more distant, but she knew she didn't dare come out.

When they became louder again, she feared that Alfie was on her trail.

Then there was silence. Except for the wind in the rushes and grasses, which could muffle a footstep.

The thrashing began again.

"What do you think you're doing?" a man's voice called.

"Chasing that damn kid," Alfie called back. "She found something . . ."

"Stop! You idiot! You've done enough clumsy, stupid things. When I want something done, I'll give the orders, do you hear?"

160

"Yes, sir. You're the boss."

"You bet I am, and I advise you to remember that."

"Yes, sir. I'll remember."

"I'm tired of your stupidity. And his too. What he ever picked an idiot like you for—and why I ever picked him—Has that idiot been back here, leaving his calling card?"

"Gee, I don't hardly think so. We been meeting at a diner way down on Route One. We been real careful Mr. Mills."

She hadn't recognized his voice. All the music was out of it.

Becky buried her head deeper into her lap.

fifteen

Becky remained crouched in the marsh. Numb from head to toe, she had lost all sense of time. Staring at a hummock in front of her, she fancied that the tide was coming in. If the tide ebbs and flows every twelve hours, how many inches in an hour would it rise. . . no peeking. . . is there anyone in this class who has the answer to that question. . .

When would it ever be safe to leave? Just because he didn't want Alfie to chase her, didn't mean he wouldn't do it himself, did it? In one split second, nice Mr. Mills had turned into an evil stranger, someone dangerous.

And she realized that he was X, that mysterious X who would do anything to get the Mermaid. Beyond that, her benumbed brain refused to go.

She was getting more and more tired, and it was getting harder and harder to listen for footsteps. Anyway, it was nicer to listen to the song of the rushes and the grasses.

Actually, she felt safe in the marsh, damp all over and chilled too, but safe. She would be safe here even in high tide, because the water would never come high enough to drown her. She was safe if he didn't find her.

Safe from what? her weary brain asked. Would he want to kill her? Kidnap her? What? And why? And if she didn't know, how could she make any plans?

She was getting sleepy, and she longed to rest her head on a hummock. But if she fell asleep and the tide came in, then she would drown in her sleep.

She'd almost forgotten about the bracelet! Very quietly she dipped it into a little pool of water and rubbed away at the dirt. As some of the dirt washed off, she could see that it was covered with a thick coat of tarnish, greenish in spots. She stared at it, hypnotized. Working it carefully, she tried it on her arm. No sooner was it on, than she quickly took it off. It was a hateful, horrid bracelet. If it had only been found sixty-five years ago . . .

Presently, she heard a whistle, a human whistle, a gay one. Could it be *him* setting a trap for her? She reasoned that it could be, and crouched still lower.

The whistle stopped, and a man's voice said, "Okay, old-timer, here we go." A dog barked wildly. "Steady, steady. Sit, sit . . ." the dog's crying, begging noises . . . "O-kay—get it." A rush through grasses . . .

It wasn't *his* voice, and it wasn't Alfie's. With

painful caution, Becky stood up on tiptoe and peered through the rushes and grasses. She saw the head of a young man in a watch hat, saw that he was following the dog with his eyes, saw that he was smiling.

A smiling young man; training a dog to retrieve on a beautiful morning, out on a beautiful marsh. What could be more innocent, more safe than that?

But there had been that other *nice* man, walking his cute little dog, and that day had been beautiful too, hadn't it?

Did she dare leave her cover? Ask for help?

The young man blew on a whistle. His smile broadened. "Good boy, good boy," he called.

She took the risk and made her way to him.

By the expression on his face, she could tell she was a sight.

"Hey there—where'd you come from?"

She pointed to the marsh.

"So I see. But I mean where did you start from? And what happened to you?"

The dog was a golden retriever, and he was sniffing around her curiously. He made up his mind and kissed her.

"I—I lost my way."

She wasn't going to tell the whole story.

"Did—did you see anyone? A boy?"

The young man was studying her. "No. I didn't see a boy."

"Or a man?"

164

"Uh—yes. Yes. I saw a man."

"Where—where'd he go?"

"The one I saw got into a car back on the road."

"A—a limousine?"

"No. Not a limousine. As a matter of fact, I think it was a Volvo. You look a wreck. Do you want to tell me what really happened?"

Becky shook her head.

"I don't have a limousine. Or a Volvo. Only a beatup old pickup truck, but would you like me to take you home?"

She nodded as vigorously as her fatigue would allow.

"Is that your bike back there?"

"Yes."

"Well, we'll put it on the truck and take you home. Where do you live?"

"In Quoneck on Old Beach Street."

He took out a bandana handkerchief.

"You're all scratched up. Let's clean you up a bit."

He dipped the handkerchief in the water and mopped her face and her arms and her hands.

"You're also shivering." He took off his jacket and threw it over her shoulders. She remembered to say thank you.

They walked back toward the dirt road, the young man, Becky, and the dog, silently. Becky looked behind her every few steps. The young man noticed this, but didn't comment.

By the time they got to his pickup truck, Becky

didn't think she was about to be kidnapped, but even if she was, she was too tired to care. The man lifted the bike onto the truck, and lifted Becky onto the seat next to him. The dog jumped in and sat beside her.

"What's the dog's name?" she asked.

"Abner."

"Hello, Abner." She leaned her head against him. She wondered if *he* had gone to the house and picked up Winky. Poor, darling Winky.

The young man drove the way he was supposed to, ten miles an hour on the narrow dirt road. When they got to the blacktop, if he turned north instead of south, what would she do? She'd ask him please not to kidnap her, that's what. She'd tell him the truth, that she was too poor to be worth kidnapping. Besides, she was also too tired to be kidnapped, that's what she'd tell him.

When they got to the blacktop, he didn't go north and he didn't go south. The Beetle was parked there, and her father hopped out and waved his arms.

"That's my father," Becky said.

The young man braked and brought the truck to a stop.

Her father ran over to the truck.

"Becky! You look terrible. What happened?"

She held up the bracelet.

"Look!" she whispered. "Look!"

"Good grief!" Her father took it from her. "Good

grief!" He pulled out a handkerchief, wrapped the bracelet in it, and put it in his jacket pocket. "But what happened? Why do you look so awful?" He helped her down from the truck.

"She says she lost her way," the young man said.

Becky poked her father hard.

"Oh—oh, well—we're new here, you see. I thank you for helping Becky. I can see she needed this lift. I appreciate this. Becky . . .?"

"Thank you a lot," she murmured.

Her father hesitated. "You from around these parts?"

"I'm in Quoneck too."

"Ah," her father said, and introduced himself. "And you are—?"

"Tom Smith."

As they walked to the Beetle, Becky heard her father repeat the name under his breath a couple of times.

"Why you doing that?" she asked.

"It's the common names like that that are hard to remember, when you need them."

"Why will you need it?"

"In case—we want him as a witness. When you tell me what happened, I may want to get back to him. Now, what did happen, Becky?"

He started the car, and they drove off.

Becky took a big, trembling breath: "Oh boy, wait till you hear!" She took another breath. "You see, I was building a brick tower . . ." she began and went on to tell him how she found the bracelet and what happened with Alfie Stone. She was too tired to make it as scary as it really had been; after a good rest, and maybe some hot cocoa, she knew she'd do better. But when it came time to tell about Mr. Mills, she had a spurt of energy.

"And then, when I was hiding in the marsh and it was all watery and for all I knew there were snapping turtles, then I found out who Mr. X was. Wait till you hear."

"X? You mean Z."

"I do not mean Z. I mean X. I mean X who wants to buy the Mermaid. You'll never guess . . ."

"For pete's sake, Becky, who *is* it?"

"Mr. Leonard Mills."

"*Mills?* Becky! Are you sure?"

"Nice clean Mr. Mills is a very bad man, Daddy. You should have heard him . . ."

And she told her father what she overheard.

"Are you sure this Stone boy called him 'boss'?"

"Of course I'm sure. And Mr. Mills told him not to forget it too. Ooh! What are we going to do when he comes to pick up Winky?"

"Now listen, Becky, if you're right about Mr. Mills, this is serious. Because I found out something about your Z man."

"You did? Who is he?"

"That limousine service is owned lock, stock, and barrel by a group of big-time racketeers the police call Laundry Inc. It's big-time stuff, very big-time indeed. They use businesses like this limousine service for the sole purpose of cleaning up dirty money. You see, they take money that was made illegally—criminally—and put it in a legitimate business. Then, when it's cleaned that way, they draw it out and use it. They're a dangerous, mean lot, and, as usual, they're hard to catch. I'm going right back to the phone and ask about Mills."

"Daddy—you think Mr. Mills is maybe the *godfather?*"

"I think he's maybe their mouthpiece—lawyer to you—in which case, what does he want with the Mermaid?"

"Is that why you came after me? When you found out about the Z man?"

"Yes. I don't know why, but a fatherly feeling came over me, that I didn't want my kid wandering around that particular place alone, not till I knew more."

Becky slid down on the seat and put her feet in their wet sneakers up on the dashboard.

"When are we going to take the bracelet up to Miss Hendrix?

"After I've called New York."

Becky began to giggle in a drowsy way.

"I'm going to Trento's this afternoon," she chanted "and I'm going to buy maybe ten big—oh, I don't know what—and I'm going to tell a tale—a Mermaid's tale to a bunch of kids—and . . ." she shouted, "they better believe me!" She sat up with a start. "But the Mermaid! Can Mr. Big-time Mouthpiece Mills get the Mermaid no matter what?"

"That, Becky, I do not know."

sixteen

Becky saw the rest of that morning through a haze of drowsiness.

There was her mother, mothering her with cocoa and a bath bubbling with the expensive salts she and Nina had given her for mother's day.

There was Winky, still there, and sniffing Abner like mad and not being remotely like a dog who could belong to a *godfather*.

And then there was her father coming into the kitchen after he'd spoken to his cop friend . . .

"Charles!" her mother cried, "sit down, you look funny."

"You better sit down. Both of you. Leonard Mills is not the godfather."

"Who is he?"

"He's the godfather's godfather. Nothing less than Mr. Big himself. Reynolds says he is probably the most powerful front the underworld has in this country. They've known about him for years—police all over the country know about him. But he's too smart, too powerful for them to have pinned anything on him yet. He keeps decidedly behind the scenes, as far as the underworld is concerned, but he makes his presence known in exceedingly high places—in both the political and the business worlds. He leads a double life, and they know he's been carefully working toward a new, quiet, elegant image—trying to separate himself from all visible ties to organized crime. Hence, the quiet respectability of Quoneck and the understated beauty of the Mermaid."

Becky pushed her cocoa away.

Her mother whispered, "Crime . . . the syndicate . . . here . . . in our house."

She began to laugh.

"Tilly—what in heaven's name . . . ?"

"Oh . . ." she mopped her eyes. "To think that our one and only friend in this whole place turns out to be the biggest mobster in the United States of America!"

"Daddy," Becky asked, "is he powerful enough to get the Mermaid, no matter what?"

"You just heard what Reynolds had to say about his power—to the highest places . . ."

Becky rested her chin in her hands. "Daddy," she murmured drowsily, "do you suppose Mr. Adams knows who Mr. Mills is?"

Her father stared at her.

"Now that, Becky, is an interesting question."

He picked the phone up.

"Charles! What are you up to?"

"I'd like to pay a call on Mr. Adams."

"Charles! I absolutely and positively refuse to let you tangle with ORGANIZED CRIME, WITH THE MAFIA!"

"Mommy, shh! Suppose Mr. Mills hears you."

"Mathilda, Becky is right. Drop your voice. And calm down."

He telephoned Mr. Adams. He said he had some information about a prospective customer; he said it was urgent. He hung up.

"He says I should come right over."

Becky went to the clothes rack on the wall and grabbed her jacket.

"Where do you think you're going, Miss?"

"With Daddy."

"Charles!" Her mother pleaded with him.

"I'm the one who found out about him first and Mr. Adams might want to ask me some questions."

Her father thought there was no danger in her going to the boat yard, and he thought Becky had earned the right to the story.

"Are we going to show him the bracelet before we take it to Miss Hendrix?"

"That's a good idea. He can begin to spread the word."

"I want to be the one to show it to him."

"Very well then," her mother said, "you can go,

both of you, but if you think I'm going to be left to face that mobster all by myself, you're crazy. I'm going too. And so is Winky."

If Mr. Adams was taken aback when he saw the whole family arrive, he was too polite and too reserved to show it. He merely fetched another chair.

Becky sat up as straight as she could, while her father told about Mr. Mills.

He took rather too long, she thought. She was impatient for him to get to the part where she found the bracelet, which, as far as she could see, was still the most important part of the story.

When he finally did get there, she had to fish through all the pockets of her jacket before she found it. It was embarrassing.

She put the bracelet down on the desk, in front of Mr. Adams. He studied it without touching it.

"In this village," he said, after a while, "we all grew up believing Hope's story."

He swivelled his chair and looked at the boats on the water.

He had listened politely to her father, never once interrupting him. Becky couldn't tell how he was taking it—Mr. Mills, the truth about the fire at the music house, any of it.

When he turned back to them, his handsome, weathered face was drawn.

"I am not going to pretend," he said, "that I am not deeply, badly shaken. As for Euphemia . . . I'm not able to talk about that yet. But Mills! I can't get over how completely taken in I was by the man. Not a false note. Great attention to detail—including the right little dog—no German shepherd or Doberman pinscher for him—the right clothes. Yes, every inch the important lawyer. Which, alas, he is. Even the style with which he sprinkled the glamorous names around. Not one of your typical, snobbish name droppers, who make you wonder whether they really do know the people they claim to. And the horror in this case is that they *do* hobnob with a Mills. Innocently—or otherwise." He looked back at the boats. "What a disgrace it is that the likes of him are loose! How frightening!"

"But—is he going to get a boat—and the Mermaid too?" Becky asked.

Mr. Adams kept on looking out the window.

"I've never in my life tangled with a mobster," he said, "and I confess it's daunting. Yes, it's daunting." He turned and gave Becky the shadow of a smile. "Becky, I'm going to try my best to persuade Mr. Mills that he would not find Quoneck an agreeable port for him. I don't imagine it would suit this new image he's working on to be surrounded by people who know too much about him. Before I lose my nerve . . ." He reached for the phone, and Becky noticed that his hand was not steady. "I'm calling Ethel Bolton at The Gull."

"Ethel? Carter Adams. Is Mr. Mills there? . . . when he comes back ask him to run over to the yard,

175

tell him I'd like to talk to him . . . yes, Ethel . . . no, Ethel, there won't be any more suspicious fires . . . incidentally, Ethel, the little girl, Becky, found Hope's bracelet up at the music house . . . yes, Becky . . . yes, it was there all the time . . . yes, Ethel, I'm looking at it right now . . . no, not at the bottom of the ocean . . . well, for heaven's sake, sit down . . . no, I don't believe it was Euphemia who set the fires . . . Oh, Ethel, this time let's leave it to the proper authorities . . . yes, yes, they'll probably question Alfie about the fires and the firing at the train too . . . What am I going to do about Euphemia? I intend to let her know how bad I feel . . . Ethel, I'm sure you want to use the phone for the rest of the morning, but please don't forget about Mr. Mills . . ."

He put the phone down slowly.

"Phew! Ethel's going to be busy spreading the news . . ."

Becky interrupted: "Daddy, we've got to get up to Miss Hendrix with the bracelet."

"It's our next stop, Becky."

Mr. Adams continued: ". . . and now all I have to do is figure out what I'm going to say to Mills." He smiled wryly. "I don't much care to have him as an enemy."

They all stood up.

With one foot out the door, Becky heard Mr. Adams thank them for coming . . . heard him admire her for going it alone . . . whole village was going to be grateful to them . . . hoped he wouldn't fail his end of it . . . wondered whether her mother wouldn't like to meet his wife over a cup of tea?

Becky was proud of her mother. She was dignified and quiet and didn't roll over and play dead because she'd just made the Adams's guest list. All she said was that it would be very pleasant.

THEY STOPPED at the entrance to the Mermaid, and Becky went up alone.

With trees and grasses waving and rippling and the sun making a play of light and shadow, the house seemed afloat and riding the wind. The mermaid was swinging gently back and forth, now east, now west, and looked pleased to have the secret finally out.

Miss Hendrix was propped up on the chaise and staring out to sea. She, herself, looked like a sad old weathervane.

Becky wondered where she would begin—with X or Z or the bracelet.

It was Miss Hendrix who made the choice.

She spotted the tarnished circle in Becky's hand. Telling about it later, Becky said it was like watching a picture of a healing miracle. Color came into the powdery white cheeks; she straightened up, and finally rose from the chaise and walked to the long window and opened it. She stood there with the bracelet in her hand, her face thrust forward into the sea air.

"Where did you find it?" she asked.

"Near the fireplace."

"So she lost it in the house itself. Why didn't I ever think of that? She must have been running around, teasing Luke before . . ." She flung the bracelet from her as if it were burning her fingers. It fell on the floor with a dull thud. "I shall wrap it up and mail it to her without writing a word. I shall send it registered mail, return receipt requested." She went over to Becky and kissed her on the forehead. "I am incredibly hungry now." She started toward the kitchen, where Pat was to be heard bustling about.

"I have more to tell you—"

"Do you? I'm not sure I can absorb anymore just yet."

"We found out that X is a man from the underworld—a great big mobster."

"Oh, Hope never was discriminating about people. It's too bad I won't see her face when she opens the package and finds the bracelet."

"He's terribly powerful, Miss Hendrix."

"Not powerful enough to buy the Mermaid, dear. Not now. Goodness, I *am* hungry. A new lease on life gives one such an appetite. Did you say mobster? How interesting. What would a mobster want with the Mermaid? You'll tell me about it later?"

Becky told her that her parents were waiting for her.

"In the afternoon then. Over a cup of tea with

cinnamon toast and strawberry jam and some tiny cucumber sandwiches too."

Becky had other plans for that afternoon.

"Is tomorrow all right?"

"Of course. And, Becky, my friend, we shall hunt fleabane together one day."

MR. MILLS came in the early afternoon.

When they heard footsteps on the paved path leading up to their house, Becky peered out a window.

"It's him," she said, and her heart began to pound painfully.

The three of them stood stiff and awkward in the kitchen, waiting for the knock.

Winky had heard him and was, as usual, wild with excitement.

He came in as if nothing had happened, smooth as silk, his voice back to musical. He allowed Winky to greet him, then quieted her. Becky thought he mustn't have been to see Mr. Adams yet.

She stole a look at his eyes, really only noticed them for the first time. The mugger's eyes had been ice cold. Mr. Mills's, she now saw, were cold too, but had fiery glints in back of the cold. His eyes scared her. She remembered what Miss Hendrix had said: ". . . the whole business smells of power, evil power . . ." Why hadn't she—or her parents—looked at his eyes before? Now, right here in their very own kitchen there was this evil power.

He looked at them, each one of them, and a flicker of amusement appeared in those eyes. Secret amusement? So he had seen Mr. Adams. Becky went cold all over.

"Becky—" He took a soft leather wallet with gold edges out of his jacket. He riffled through the bills in them. "Do you like new money? Clean money?" He smiled his friendly, open smile.

"Uh—uh—uh . . ."

"Here's a nice, new crisp bill." It was a ten dollar bill. "Will that do?"

She had never been so tongue-tied, and she couldn't even nod.

"Now, my dear, I have serious business to discuss with you." He glanced at his watch. "Unfortunately, I'm pressed for time."

Her father spoke. His voice was strange, tight. "Is this—this business with Becky? Or is it with us?"

Mr. Mills raised his eyebrows. "Oh—please—I didn't mean to be impolite. It's with all of you. No secrets. I was wondering how Becky would like to keep Champion Windermere's Duchess of York? To have as her own dog?"

"*Winky? Mine?*"

Her father spoke again. "Just a minute. Winky is a very expensive dog . . ."

"Oh, come now, what difference does that make?"

"It—could—"

Mr. Mills laughed softly. "There are no strings attached. I promise you. You see—my plans are changed. I have decided not to take a charter here after all."

"Oh."

Becky wasn't sure, but she thought they'd all said it together.

He smiled and spoke ironically: "Confidentially, I perceive that Quoneck does not take kindly to outsiders—like us."

He looked at his watch again.

"Do let the child keep the dog. They suit each other."

Becky held her breath while her parents exchanged looks.

"Please . . . ?" she begged. "*I* love Winky." They nodded.

Becky was on the floor with Winky when she heard Mr. Mills say "My card—if I can ever introduce your daughter Nina to people in the theater or film."

She heard her parents mumbling, and her mother saying, in a frozen voice, "Becky, you haven't thanked Mr. Mills for Winky."

He said it wasn't necessary and that he really had to run.

They waited for him to be safely gone before they dared open their mouths.

Her mother said, "What gall!"

Her father spoke slowly, carefully. "No, Tilly, it *wasn't* gall. He's beyond needing to display gall. That would mean that he cared. He doesn't care.

About anything, but power. The rest is all a joke to him. *We're* nothing but jokes. All decent people are jokes. And in his book, Nina would be stupid not to get help wherever she can find it. If necessary, in the gutter. You see—he just couldn't be bothered putting up a fight here. There are plenty of other villages to go to. And he won't use the Z man again. He was too visible, too clumsy, and too stupid. Ironically, Z too was an outsider and didn't know how to operate here. He should never have picked an inexperienced little hoodlum like Alfie for what was essentially a subtle job. Thank goodness he did. Oh, Mills will go on."

Becky added, outraged, "And he could give Winky away as if she was nothing but a—a tie that didn't match!" She picked herself up from the floor, picked Winky up, and, with a sudden change of mood, began to dance around the kitchen singing: "Riddle me, riddle me, riddle me ree, the Mermaid's safe as safe can be . . ."

There are no secrets in Quoneck.

When Becky walked into Trento's that afternoon, Van and Clarissa and Peggy and two or three other kids were already there. Her timing, as she had meant it to be, was good.

Peggy was the one who spoke first.

She said: "Gee!"

And Clarissa said: "You want one of my Mary Janes?"

Becky accepted it with thanks, and they all watched as she bit into it. Becky smiled at them; they smiled back. Someone giggled.

"Feel like telling us what happened?" Peggy asked.

Becky nodded.

They made themselves comfortable, off to one side near a rack of comics. Becky grinned and began:

"You know where the marsh is . . ."

They appreciated her joke, and she continued, "I was just doodling with some bricks, trying to build a tower . . ."

What with one thing and another, she didn't get home till suppertime, and she could barely eat it she was so excited. She was going to Peggy's the next afternoon to listen to some new records. Some of the other kids would be dropping in. If Peggy's mother had enough stew, could she stay for supper? Why not? her mother wanted to know.

"I think I'm going to buy a new tea kettle . . ." her mother said, dreamily.

Her father smiled. "Before I get a new job?"

"Oh, you'll get one eventually," her mother answered, airily.

The phone rang and her father answered it.

He listened solemnly and, still solemn, he said: "Thank you for calling. I'll come fetch him immediately."

He came back to the table and went on eating.

What was *that* about? they demanded.

With a straight face, her father answered: "Oh, that was a boy who said, 'Sir, your horse is in our garden.' "

"But we don't have a horse," said Becky's mother.

"Don't we?"

"You know we don't, Charles."

Becky giggled. "Daddy, do you think . . .?"

"Yes, I'm pretty sure that was our sinister, anonymous caller. And if I'm not mistaken, he has just made his last call."